Lord Teignmouth

Lays Lyrical and Legendary Ballads and Paraphrases

Ballads and Paraphrases

Lord Teignmouth

Lays Lyrical and Legendary Ballads and Paraphrases
Ballads and Paraphrases

ISBN/EAN: 9783744777650

Printed in Europe, USA, Canada, Australia, Japan

Cover: Foto ©Andreas Hilbeck / pixelio.de

More available books at www.hansebooks.com

LAYS

LYRICAL AND LEGENDARY,

BALLADS

AND

PARAPHRASES.

BY

LORD TEIGNMOUTH.

LONDON:

E. MOXON, SON & CO., DOVER STREET.

1869.

LONDON :

SWIFT AND CO., REGENT PRESS, KING STREET,

REGENT STREET, W.

PREFACE.

OF the following Poems, composed on various occasions during many years, and subsequently revised, some have already appeared in print.

Langton Hall, Northallerton.
Dec. 6th, 1869.

CONTENTS.

I.

TO TWILIGHT.

1814.

ERRATA.

Page 55, line 11, *read* "speeds" *for* "sped.
„ 70, „ 17, *read* "pranks" *for* "freaks."
„ 103, „ 15, *read* "ancestry" *for* "ancestors."
„ 112, „ 5, *read* "bays" *for* "days.
„ 137, „ 11, *read* "heads" *for* "leads.'

Sweet as the breeze 'mid Afric's summer glow ;
Sweet to the man, whose weary task is done,
Who with the sun his daily course has run,
Whom social greetings welcome to the board
His toils supply, the couch his fields afford ;
While conscience broods not on the day misspent,
And o'er his closing eye-lids breathes content.

I.

TO TWILIGHT.

1814.

THE charms of Solitude,—the slumbering lake,—
The melody of water, breeze and brake,—
The shepherd's homeward steps,—the sheepfold's
     bell,—
Light's parting ray, and Nature's mute farewell,
Are thine, loved Twilight;—sweet the lonely
     scene,
Calm as religion, as content serene ;
Scene of reflection, to the toil-worn brow
Sweet as the breeze 'mid Afric's summer glow ;
Sweet to the man, whose weary task is done,
Who with the sun his daily course has run,
Whom social greetings welcome to the board
His toils supply, the couch his fields afford ;
While conscience broods not on the day misspent,
And o'er his closing eye-lids breathes content.

B

But the poor wanderer as thy shades advance,
As lingers yet the day,—hope's parting glance,
Hastes to the vale,—frown dark'ning woods
    around;
Hastes to the hill, yet hills the prospect bound,
Till clóuds o'er clouds, o'er shadows shadows roll,
And light's last gleam has faded on the soul:
Houseless and friendless on the dewy soil
He spreads his shivering limbs, and rests from toil.

Twilight of life, thy deepening shades impart
A solemn influence to the dying heart.
Say, wearied pilgrim of the troubled day,
Say, ere life's fleeting visions roll away,
Did noon-day toil thy feverish brow bedew,
Have cares been many, and have joys been few?
When morning smiled, and hope was on the
    wing,
Did sage reflection o'er thy bosom spring?
And did'st thou check thy joys, thy follies leave
To muse on passing hours and toil for eve?
Then pilgrim rest, the couch thy youth has spread
Shall soothe thy tott'ring limbs, thine aching head:
Rest, rest, in hope till on thy sleep shall break
A brighter day, and heav'n shall bid thee wake.
But ah when age knows not reflection's pow'r
Till fades the day, till Twilight's awful hour,

From scene to scene when thoughtless youth has
    roved,
And man still hates the scenes that youth had loved,
Flies from his home, and changeful Fortune's
    child
Unsated roams, from clime to clime beguiled,
When on each devious path alike by youth
Or manhood trodden beams the light of truth,
While lingers thought on joys he may not share,
In that dread hour, he owns, of dark despair,
Had youth reflected, manhood toiled and wept,
Twilight had whispered peace, and age had slept.
But the last fainting ray of hope has fled,
And waits his doom the unrepenting dead.

II.
TRUE AND FALSE PHILOSOPHY.

WHEN man, by native wisdom taught,
Deems this vain world a thing of nought,
And all its pleasure, pomp and power
The fleeting visions of an hour,
With scorn he sees the giddy crowd
Or madly weep, or laugh aloud,
In secret anguish doomed to drain
His cup of pleasure or of pain.

For him the day no joyaunce brings,
It doth but gild Time's hastening wings,
And as in mockery bestow
Its splendour on a world of woe.
For him the night oblivion woos
In vain, since Death her form pursues;
The image of his lost repose
Appals him ere his eyelids close.

To man a foe he treads awhile
His lonely path, by heavenly smile
Uncheered : self-sated then he flies
To Nature's genial sympathies :
Borne by the fury of his mind
Where rolls the wave, or wafts the wind,
Like wandering spirit of the air,
He seeks the converse of despair.

Ah, whither, captive, dost thou roam ?
Has life no haven, man no home ?
And dost thou think thy torturer fell,
Who dooms thee to his native hell,
And still thy faltering steps doth urge
O'er howling waste and foaming surge,
Shall lead thee to some still retreat,
For seraphs' high communion meet ?

And wilt thou nurse thine inborn guest,
The hidden vulture of thy breast,
With stupor fierce or joy accurst
Cling to the chains thou canst not burst,
Or fainting sue with penance vain
The phantom-idols of thy brain?
E'en now beneath thee yawns the grave,—
They fly, those gods who cannot save.

Yet hark, amid the thunder's sound
That rolls athwart the gulf profound,
A still small voice that whispers peace,
That bids thy toil, thy warfare cease,
And tells thee of a beacon-light
That mocks the day, dispels the night:
The light within thy bosom glows,
From thence the living lustre flows.

And oh, how chang'd those scenes, of late
To thy dim eyes so desolate!
How bright those hills once wrapt in gloom,
How fair those vales' renascent bloom:
Those transient forms, that mock'd the view
When clad in folly's tinsel hue,
In new and borrow'd lustre shine,—
" The hand that made them is Divine."

All Nature feels the sweet control,
In festal pomp the seasons roll ;
The star of morning smiles serene,
And day with rapture crowns the scene ;
The eve more calm delight inspires,
Night wakes devotion's holier fires ;
The soul responsive hears their voice,
And joyous bids the world rejoice.

The lamp of heaven shall never die,
For hands unseen its light supply :
The passing suns may shade its beam,
But cannot quench the living stream ;
The clouds and midnight damps obscure :
It glows yet more intensely pure,
And shall its shattered rays renew,
Though winds assail or storms subdue.

And when in browner Twilight fade
Life's waning gleams and lengthening shade,
And Death, enrobed in pall of night,
Tears the faint landscape from thy sight ;
The star that ruled thy morning prime
Shall cheer the eve of parting time,
In glory deepening gloom array,
Nor set but in immortal day.

III.

THE FROGS.

A Penseroso FOR WORDSWORTH'S *Allegro,*
" THE DAFFODILS."

" I wander'd lonely as a cloud."

LONELY as marsh light of the brake
   I roam'd with dank mist choking,
Where, spawn unblest of a stagnant lake,
   Ten thousand frogs lay croaking.

And 'twas a rueful sight to see
   How throbbed each straining throat
Of that belated company
   Amid the sedge afloat :

As 'twere the wailing of the daughters
   Of some amphibious fay,
Who sang amid those slimy waters
   The dirge of the dying day :

Or as if when the scorching wind
  Had dried the boundless flood,
Some spirits accurst had tarried behind,
  And groan'd from their grave of mud.

The moon was up, but the morass
  No sweet reflection gave,
For tangled weeds and clotted grass
  Did o'er its surface wave.

The shades broke in, and twitter'd by
  The bat on his noiseless wing,
And the frogs they croaked more horribly
  Than I have power to sing.

The night-jar too wheeled round and round,
  And shrilly shrieked anon ;—
I shook as 'twere Tartarean ground
  That I did tread upon.

Chilly and damp the breeze it blew,
  And my skin turned icy cold,
And methought at last it slimy grew,
  And shrivelly to behold.

And rang with louder peals the fen
  Than it ever rang before :

I gave one croak myself, and then
Fled that ill-fated shore.

But, oh, how chastening was that thrill
Of soul-subduing fear;
The fen's harsh discord vibrates still
In wisdom's inward ear.

When buoyant on the gales of morn
I taste too free a joy,
Forgetful that I was not born   .
To mirth without alloy;

Or sportive on the fumes of tea,
And skimming o'er its stream,
My spirits catch a transient glee
To speed the labouring theme,

My fancy to that loathsome lake
With putrid air half choking,
Its solitary path doth take,
And with the frogs sits croaking.

IV.

LINES.

WRITTEN FOR A SALE OF USEFUL AND ORNAMENTAL
WORK IN BEHALF OF AN INFANT SCHOOL AT
SIDMOUTH. 1828.

A SALE, a sale ! come rich and poor,
    Your grateful offerings bring ;
We've spread forth many a shining lure
    Might tempt an Eastern king.

A sale, a sale ! come, gentles, come,
    And quit each soft retreat,
Nor let the cares or joys of home
    Divert your willing feet.

From Sid's bright vale, from Paccomb long
    Famed seat of ancient lore ;
From Salcomb, where the Muses' song
    Blends with the ocean's roar ;

From the green glades and shady dells,
  Where silent Otter flows;
Where Bicton o'er the landscape swells,
  And wealth and power repose;

From Exe, on whose dark rolling tide
  Majestic navies float,
And lordly pomp and churchman's pride
  Frown lofty and remote ;

From Dawlish, on whose shingly strand
  Slumbers the whisp'ring wave,
And nymphs from many a distant land
  Their flowing tresses lave ;

From Teign's lov'd haunts, where ever gleams
  The morning's earliest ray,
And linger long the latest beams
  Of slow declining day;

From Babycomb's huge marble pile,
  From Tor's encircling coast,
Come, gentles, come, of Britain's Isle,
  The brightest gems we boast.

The livelong day, the shortening eve
  Our task we still pursued ;

Still busy fancy did conceive,
  And still our toil renew'd.

Here garments proof 'gainst wear and tear,
  May at cheap rate be bought ;
Here scarfs of finest gossamer
  Our curious hands have wrought.

For generations yet unborn
  We've woven soft attire ;
These caps a princess might adorn,
  And bid a court admire.

A gown behold, like fruitful ground
  With spangling dew-drops wet,
These flounces add like pales around
  A young plantation set.

These ribbons, if you'll purchase,—Time
  Hath not impair'd their hue,—
Not Scotland's hills in Autumn's prime
  Shall wave with bells so blue.

Then let this shawl your graceful shape
  With love-knots true entwine,
Its folds the vine's festoons shall ape,
  Or amorous eglantine.

Last round your head this bonnet bind,
  Within its vast embrace
The rays shall gather, and the wind
  Forget its wanton race.

When mirror'd in Sid's lucid tide
  Its yellow radiance spreads
The dandelions in their pride
  Shall hide their humbled heads :

And insect quires their bowers forsake,
  To blend a roundelay
With the sweet warblings of the brake,
  To greet thee Queen of May.

See here what variegated stores
  In sparkling medley strown
Shine like the mine's collected ores
  From Chili's mountain throne.

Work-bags and boxes, furnished all
  With implements complete,
Of mouldings various, great and small,
  With Tunbridge wares compete :

Watch-chains and purses, brooches, pins,
  Rosettes of gorgeous hues,

And New-year's gifts in Russian skins
   Their perfumes rich diffuse.

And pray yon bright parterre behold,
   Its flowers of matchless dye,
And woven on a ground of gold
   A scene of Arcady. .

Upon your wintry hearth spread out
   Its tints new lustre yield,
And the cricket there shall frisk about
   Like his brethren of the field.

A footstool such as this were meet
   For Papal foot, when bare
It doth the sacred college greet
   With courtesy sweet and rare.

From hearts benign these treasures flowed:
   From Avarice' sordid heap
They filtered not : Love toiling sowed,
   Let Love the harvest reap.

No grovelling thought in masquerade
   Prompts us your wealth to share,
'Tis infancy demands your aid
   And claims our fostering care :

To summon from the strife and din
  Of life's tumultuous chase,
Ere yet inured to woe and sin,
  Chilhood's untutor'd race.

For lo, on tottering limbs they run
  Each glittering prize to grasp,
Untaught the headlong steep to shun,
  Or fly th' envenom'd asp.

Too early trained in passion's school,
  By wrath and hate impelled,
They nurse for rapine and misrule
  Their spirits yet unquelled,

And born to lisp in Nature's quire
  Of praise th' adoring theme
And tune the seraph's hallowed lyre,
  Their Maker's name blaspheme.

For such poor nurslings of despair
  Your generous aid we crave,
Ere yawn for those whom Christ would spare
  The unrelenting grave.

Though moth and rust these gauds destroy,
  And fruitless seem our toil,
The seeds we sow shall spring in joy,
  Since heavenly is the soil.

THE MENAI BRIDGE.

1828.

HAIL, matchless monument of trophied Time,
Of skill divine to short lived mortals giv'n,
That, poised on wings aerial, mountest sublime,
Spanning yon channel broad, the pathless Heav'n:
As if when man, of Eden reft, had striven
With chaos stern and dread, some wizard hand
Had bound the rocky coasts asunder riven
By ocean's warring waves with magic wand,
Linking yon lonely isle for aye to fairyland.

How frail its pendent tracery appears,
When ebbs day's glory in the western sky !
Such spectral fabric sportive fancy rears,
Weaving with light's last rays of many a dye
Its shadowy web, that mocks the gazer's eye,
While to and fro, a fitful pageant, gleam
Along its line such forms as seers descry,
Where rolls on Hebrid isles th' Atlantic stream,
Hovering,   while   twilight   fades,   around   the
    waning beam.

Their phantom speed how noiseless: the sea blast
Is still, but when it heaves the surge below,
And dimly thro' the gloom yon girdle vast
Looms, as by tempests rent Heav'n's glittering bow,
Then, pilgrim, strange delight thy soul shall know
To scale its dizzy height, when the winds sweep
Its massive chains, and lightnings round thee
    glow,
And the loud thunder peals from steep to steep,
And answers from afar the hoarse resounding deep.

And haply, as when mightier spells of yore
The welkin shook, upon thine ear may thrill
The harp's wild tones; for oft on Arvon's shore,
Or Mona's cavern'd rocks, or mystic hill,
'Tis said its mournful echoes linger still.
And will no daring hand awake again
Its slumbering chords, albeit could nought instil
Of patriot ardour* thine avenging strain,
Granta's majestic bard, of Albion's later reign ?

Yes, hark, as in old Cambria's storied days,
Hall of renown, dread shrine, and fabled tow'r,
And mountain vocal with triumphant lays,
And haven, stately town, and lordly bower;

---

* Taken by poetic license from a past Welsh point of view.

While hands, that ne'er had soil'd a crimsoned
   dower,
For conquering science' brow the wreath entwine,
And cliffs that owned not Rome's usurping power,
Or Norman Edward's, Telford, welcome thine :—
All hail thy bloodless boon, and Tudor's royal line !

Yet, Telford, thou wert born in low degree,
Nor kings their homage to thy cradle brought :
Thine was the soul's innate nobility,
In patience nurtured, and by suffering taught,
The head that fashioned, and the hand that
   wrought,
The heart that loved the right, and spurned the
   wrong,
The steadfast will, th' indomitable thought,
The gentle sway, the faith* that nerves the
   strong :—
Why lacks thine high emprize the meed of death-
   less song ?

---

* See Smiles's " Lives of Engineers," Vol. II. p. 458.

VI.

HISTORICAL FRAGMENT.

1828.*

HAIL ! matchless, monument of trophied time,
Of skill divine to short lived mortals giv'n,
That o'er the Menai's strait exaltest sublime
  Thy stately pile and climbest the pathless
  Heaven !

The links, how ponderous of thy massive chain,
  Yet seeming light as wrought by fairy's hand
Or as if he of Cambria's ancient reign
  Had bound the rocky coasts with magic wand.

---

* Composed during a pedestrian tour in Wales, which accounts
for the historical events referred to being regarded from a past Welsh
point of view.   The partial remodelling of the opening stanzas of
the " Menai Bridge" in the following lines arose from a wish to
adapt the metre to a plan more extensive than that originally
proposed.

How frail thy pendent tracery appears,
  When in the western sky day's splendours ebb ;
Such airy fabric sportive fancy rears
  Weaving with light's last rays her shadowy web.

The passing forms along thy line that float
  Of car or steed the untutored wight might deem
Such spectres as amazed in isles remote
  The pilgrim views beneath the waning beam.

In vain thy bulwarks, as prevails the blast,
  Beats the pent ocean heaving to and fro :
Unmoved amid the shock thy girdle vast
  Spans the wild surge that idly chafes below.

And Mona's wondering sons no more may boast
  Freedom's loved sanctuary and holiest shrine ;
The cliffs that mocked th' imperial Roman's boast,
  Or the stern Norman's, Telford, stoop to thine.

Rolls to and fro the briny stream along
  From sea to sea, or mirror'd as a lake,
Or straitened as a torrent fierce and strong,
  Whose murmurs hoarse the caverned echoes
    wake.

What varied scenes the winding shores adorn
Of sloping lawn, dark wood, or craggy steep,
While glance from mountain tops the beams of morn
On isles far-shadowed, and the boundless deep.

Nor spread unpeopled solitudes around,
Nor hills untrodden, nor unmeasured waves ;
Man's spirit moves o'er all the scene unbound,
Nor tyrants rage, nor crouch submissive slaves.

Ev'n where round giant Snowdon's towering head
Trails the grey mist and raves the wintry wind,
The hardy shepherd owns his lowly shed,
And flocks a sweet, tho' scanty, pasture find.

While from dark nook and soft sequestered dale
The peaceful hamlet's jocund voices rise ;
And o'er Llanberris' lake or Ogwen's vale
Frown time-worn turrets from the murky skies.

Where gathering breakers of the treacherous shoal,
And shrieking sea-mews warn the venturous bark,
Rugged and scathed, as from the deep some knoll
By storms upheaved, Carnarvon's ramparts mark.

Of strange vicissitudes still sadly tell
Those solemn tow'rs ; of conquests dearly won,

Of victory's shouts and sorrow's answering knell,
The sire triumphant, and the murdered son.

Nor less, where Northward yon bluff headland rears
Its shadowy cliffs o'er Conway's foaming flood,
Points the dim Spectre of forgotten years
To sands and billows dyed with patriot blood.

Seek, pilgrim, as I've sought, yon roofless halls,
Where sullen homage own'd the Norman sway,
When the storm's lurid blaze enwraps those walls,
Whence flash'd of old from shields and spears
the day,

And thunders rock the tottering tow'rs, alone
To list of ages past the mournful dirge
Of howling winds imprisoned, to the moan
Responsive of hill blast and distant surge.

And as thy footfall's echoes in the gate,
Now mute to clang of arms and captive's chain,
Sound as the knell of conquest's crimsoned state,
Ambition's hope and glory's triumph vain,

Turn sadden'd, while thy day dreams fade anew,
From storied pageantry of weal or woe

Where tow'rs for ever brightening on the view
Unsunned arise and living waters flow.

But themes sublime by seraph quires be sung ;
    Whither, too daring Muse, aspires thy flight ?
To such may Cambria's harp be ever strung,
    And on her bards descend celestial light.

Deep in yon bay, whose wood-crowned turrets bend
    O'er the broad beach, to seamen tempest-tost
A haven dear, Beaumaris' walls extend,
    Bright gem of fabled Mona's dreary coast.

Where on the horizon's verge the billows roll,
    See smiling Commerce greet her welcome sails
From the scorched tropics bound or frozen Pole,
    From Greenland's snows or India's torrid gales.

Blithely they haste in Britain's lap to pour
    Of tributary realms the well-earned spoil ;
Realms which ne'er saw Rome's conquering eagles
        soar,
Or Venice' dreaded lion flout the soil.

Again to earth's remotest shores they roam,
    And trackless seas and starless skies defy,

Where the tusked walrus guards her icy dome,
And midnight howlings bode the tempest nigh.

Go daring barks, with keels resistless still
   Thro' storm and darkness plough th' unfathomed
      deep,
Triumphant Britain's destinies fulfil,
   And bid her banner wave, her thunder sleep.

Fair Ocean Queen, in arts and arms supreme,
   Loved of the free, the beauteous and the brave,
Throned on thine isles, who see'st thy pennon
      stream,
   Where'er the breezes waft or rolls the wave ;

Exulting in thy wide imperial sway,
   As if thy brow by deathless wreaths were bound,
Thy power pervading as the solar ray,
   Yet stable as the rocks that gird thee round ;

Forgetful that but yester-eve beheld
   Embattled nations leagued against thy life ;
While hope awhile her trembling ray withheld
   From that dark hour of agonizing strife,

When dauntless still from thine unerring bow,
   On many a sea renowned and many a plain,

Thou spedst the shaft that laid Gaul's despot low,
And Europe, bursting from her broken chain,

Hailed while she saw thy meteor standard furled,
Thy milder beam's bland influence, and from far
Columbia owned thee of a rescued world
The Cynosure, and Freedom's morning star;

And that, ere dawn the fated morrow's morn,
Some monstrous birth of Time's portentous
womb
May mark thee for his prey by factions torn,
And nations rise to ratify thy doom.

For Empire, restless as the fleeting cloud
That wings from hill to hill its heavenward way,
Here roams reluctant guest, while vainly proud
Of homage brief man woos her fickle stay.

Of realms to ruin by her smile betrayed
What mournful phantoms swell the shadowy
train—
Who lordly once like thee the sceptre swayed,
And launch'd their fleets victorious on the main :

Great Nineveh, whose pride high heaven defied
And blasted fell : and Babylon no more

Her stars invoking: drooping side by side
The sister queens of Syria's palmy shore :

Egypt, oppressor stern, by heav'n abhorred,
And Persia ev'n for glory clad with shame :
And mighty Macedon, whose conquering sword
On Asia flashed like heav'n's own shaft of flame :

Majestic Rome, who in her vast embrace
Gathered all nations and decreed their doom,
And from her teeming womb a motley race
Of kingdoms towering in the twilight gloom :

And thence emerging other States, who still
Instinct with youth, or renovated might,
Or shorn of ancient strength, the Almighty will
Fulfilling hasten to the shades of night.

Lettered on shifting sands their names, be thine
On rock of adamant for ever sure
Fair Britain, graven, while, hymned on harps divine,
Deeds wrought in faith may angel hosts allure

To lead thy van of battle where afar
O'er ocean, isle or realms of old renown,
Or yet unsung, thy sons, in bloodless war
Still conquering, greet th' incorruptible crown.

To mortal ken how few, to faith's keen eye
Each rears the banner of a host unseen,
Innumerous as the stars that gem the sky,
Or sands that glitter in the solar sheen ;

On earth still militant, till He of life
And light eternal Lord shall from his throne
The usurper hurl, bid nations cease from strife,
And from the sated grave redeem his own.

He comes ! along thy wild and wave-worn steep,
Britain, by seers foretold, what glory streams !
Thy watchmen not in vain their vigils keep,
The Sun is risen, they hail his orient beams ;

The Sun of Righteousness, whose dawning ray
Pierced the dark mists that wrapped thee, from
the gloom
Chasing hell's sullen brood where rife they lay,
With ruthless carnage glutted : meet their doom.

Dread Mona, land of woe, dark Druid isle,
Idolatry's stern nurse, disclose thy slain,
Whose hell-devoted life-blood steeped the soil,
Where yon grey stones bestrew the heathery plain.

In pillared pomp, concentric once they rose,
  A rugged roofless pile, a temple rude :
High in the midst thy priest with oak-wreathed
    brow
  And snowy vest in holy frenzy stood.

With many a mystic rite and muttered prayer
  He spread the sacrifice, the victim bound,
Then grasped the knife with arm for slaughter
    bare ;
  Groans rent the air and human blood flow'd
    round.

O vain atonement, foulest deadliest deed
  By demon hate devised, by heav'n accurst,
Long on thy fathers and their fated seed
  Of wrath divine the fiery tempest burst.

War yoked his furious steeds, and scoured the plain,
  O'erthrew the altars, and the forest felled :
But Albion soon amidst his conqu'ring train
  A form of meekest, lowliest mien beheld.

'Twas earthly, and a simple garb she wore,
  Yet all celestial was her heavenward look,
Her fair right hand a wand of myrtle bore,
  Her left devoutly pressed the sacred book :

And still she spoke of peace in accents mild,
  Of ceasing discord and triumphant love,
Of God to pardoned sinners reconciled,
  And joys unfading in the realms above.

The stalwart chief leaned listening from his car,
  And bade his serried ranks the tidings hear,
And monarchs radiant from victorious war,
  Approved her wisdom, gentle tho' severe.

Down iron cheeks the tear of pity stole,
  Victors and vanquished one true God adored,
Of equal laws obeyed the just control,
  And Alfred bowed the knee.or grasped the sword.

Then Albion free, and great and glorious rose,
  Conquered, yet conquering still her sceptre reared,
Her Norman monarchs crushed her stubborn foes,
  Knelt at her shrines, her ancient laws revered.

  * * * * * *

On Cambria's hills the beacon blaze of war!
  It gleams on wizard stream and mystic vale,
On hallowed homes, and fanes revered afar,
  While tracks th' invader's march the voice of
  wail.

On Arvon's shores his glittering ranks behold,
    Avail nor fierce despair nor suppliant charms;
The Saxon wins thee as thy seers foretold,
    Land of the free-born, to his conquering arms.

And on the mound where late sublime they stood
    In strife's last hour amid thy rallying bands,
While Menai's surging eddies drank their blood,
    And corses rife strewed Mona's golden sands,

A glorious choir in flowing robes arrayed,
    Their hoar locks streaming to the troubled wind,
Reckless of volleying shaft or quivering blade,
    Spurning the yoke; to gory death resigned,

While still they hymned, in descant wild and high,
    Till ebbing life's last gasp dear freedom's name,
And dying 'mid celestial minstrelsy
    Soared heavenward in the martyr's car of flame,

There of thy bards the mangled relics lay,
    Nor unavenged;—where Snowdon rears serene
His mountain throne, 'tis said in bright array
    Dire harbingers of woe their forms were seen;

And on the monarch's ear, while homeward wound
    His trophied host around the mountain's base,

O'er flood and fell, above, beneath, around,
  Pealed the loud doom of Edward's fated race.

In vain of mustering bands arose the clang,
  The servile shout that hailed triumphant wrong:
In vain thro' Ryddlan's hall at midnight rang
  The revel high and blazed the festal throng :

In vain all radiant from her stately towers
  On valour's deeds approving Beauty smiled,
Or soft retired in Clwidd's blooming bow'rs
  War's stern resolve with love's delights beguiled;

The curse still urged, and time hath sealed its doom,
  And still its echoes shall thy chords prolong,
The curse which sleeps not in the silent tomb,
  The curse immortal of avenging song,

Granta's majestic bard ! The prophet's car,
  The azure fields of light and steeds of fire
Were thine: thy course I follow from afar,
  While wakes no meaner theme my feebler lyre.

Mona I sing and Tudor's royal line !
  O'er grim oppression's woes and grinding chains
Say, Cambria, shall thy sons for ever pine,
  Nor wake thy silent harp's forgotten strains ?

Lo ! on thy mountains of tyrannic sway,
    No trophies hoar the mantling mists enfold :
It blazed and vanished like the meteor's ray,
    While tower their summits proudly as of old :

As when 'mid tempest's howl and torrent's roar,
    Wandering and wild, their guide the western sun,
From ravening wolf, rude elk, and brindled boar,
    Their stormy holds thy sires primeval won,

And from their rugged battlements defied
    The bold Phœnician, while in long array
His galleys bounded blithely o'er the tide
    From " waves that rock the cradle of the day : "

Or when from that dread Spirit shrank the eye,
    Whose glance from Ind to Lusitania's strand
Flashed, as ill-omen'd from the sultry sky
    On guilty nations Sirion's flaming brand :

Spirit of freedom spurning man's control,
    Whose converse high thy prophet bards inspired,
From earthborn care and passion purged the soul,
    And with the love of deathless glory fired,

Till of immortal essence they partook,
    Of harmony insphered and mystic power,

And bowed by Modred's spells the mountains shook,
And ocean own'd the might of dark Glendow'r ;

And to enraptured strains thine harp was
   strung,
Ere yet thy bards Llewellyn mourn'd in vain,
Nor mute the chords, and vocal was the tongue
   That lulled the winds and hushed the stormy
   main ;

Vocal no more, save where on lonely hill
   At night's calm noon, aërial minstrelsy
Around the sod sepulchral lingers still ;
   Or when, as of old time, the warrior cry

Told Albion that thy Tudor's call awoke
   The spirit of thy sons, and from afar
Rush'd forth their bands, by vengeance fired, and
   broke
Full on her sheep-clad plains the blast of war.

In vain usurping York his might withstood,
   Bulwarks high towered and Bosworth's stern
   array,
And Albion sheathed her sword with kindred blood
   Yet red, and blessed her British Tudor's sway.

Ev'n as when severed from the shattered side
   Of Alp or Apennine some craggy knoll

D

O'erwhelms the vale, in desolation wide
 Rocks piled on rocks and mingled forests roll :

From hill to hill upheaved a rampart towers,
 And chafes the torrent pent and swoll'n, by rills
Innumerous fed and snows and frequent show'rs,
 Till the vast chasm the growing burthen fills.

Hamlets deep-fathomed lie, the voices hushed,
 And notes of joy that hail'd the blooming morn,
And fitful din of cataracts that gushed
 From steep to steep, as if since Time was born

Lonely and dark and deep that lake had slept,
 And save when ruffled by the wolf's gaunt brood,
Or cygnet's plash, or by the wild wind swept,
 All motionless as Death's unaltered mood.

When hark from the abyss, as if by throes
 Convulsive Earth were rent, a sullen roar !
The cloven mound the surging tide o'erflows ;
 A moment smiles the landscape, and no more ;

To the far hills the flocks in dire dismay
 Fly, while forlorn and reft the weeping swain
Seeks, where rank sedge and miry reed betray
 The watery waste, his sire's loved cot in vain.

But Spring hath waved her brooding wings anew,
   Homesteads arise and fanes their turrets rear,
Fresh verdure glitters in the morning dew,
   And ampler harvests crown the exulting year.

  *   *   *   *   *

Cradled in woe, a virgin queen is born,—
   In her pale cheek care blights the opening rose :
Avaunt ye clouds that blacken o'er her morn,
   The noon-day splendour of her realm disclose !

To Wisdom's voice a willing ear she bends,
   And Justice lifts aloft her golden scales,
And Faith's pure incense from her shrines ascends,
   While haughty Rome her empire lost bewails.

See jocund Peace lead on the laughing hours,
   And smiling Plenty cheer the lab'ring swain ;
The joyous Muse repairs her broken bow'rs,
   And hark on Avon's banks th' immortal strain !

Eliza's fame shall bards unborn resound,
   And tell how fared the huge Armada's pride,
How Raleigh grasped the sword in myrtle bound,
   And Sidney sweetly sang and nobly died.

But oh what star malign its lustre flings
  To blight the promise of that glorious hour;
What spectres wan of slain or vanquished kings,
  And queens discrowned in shadowy distance
  lower!

Ill-fated line, could blood for crimes atone,
  Dark Flodden had appeased Heav'n's vengeful
  ire,
And Mary loath no more in chains to groan
  Had blessed the axe that bade the curse expire.

The sword that o'er the sire suspended gleams
  Upon the son's devoted head shall fall :
Lo, on the block a monarch's life-blood streams,
  And mad Sedition hails th' usurper's throne.

To vengeance cries the son and fires the war :
  On Worcester's fated field he turns the rein,
And roams a helpless fugitive afar
  To mourn his trampled crown and nobles slain.

But destined yet a happier lot to prove,
  Dash from thy lips the chalice of despair :
A late-repentant people's tardy love
  Recalls thee to a throne of thorny care :

And o'er the stones, but yesterday bedew'd
  By thy sire's murder, rolls thy car elate,

And with foul rapine gorged, Rebellion's brood
　Their surfeit loathe, and hail thy royal state.
●
Now glorious is the task that waits thee, child
　Of sad vicissitudes and countless wrongs ;
Be not by fortune's treacherous smiles beguiled ;
　To thee the patriot's sterner part belongs.

In the fierce furnace of affliction tried,
　And constant found, behold a faithful band,
Friends of thy sire, brave Ormond, generous Hyde,
　And Monk, 'mid factions dauntless, round thee
　　stand.

A nation's crime a monarch must forgive,
　Heav'n can alone a nation's forfeit claim ;
Restore thine exiles, bid thy captives live,
　And cherish loyalty's undying flame ;

Thy tott'ring throne, that rests on Freedom's base,
　From secret plots, from hostile arms defend ;
So shall thy brows unfading laurels grace,
　And to thy prayers shall Heav'n propitious bend.

But lighter cares thy reckless thoughts employ ;
　On wanton Pleasure's flowery lap reclined
Thou deemest thy sceptre but a glitt'ring toy,
　And yieldest to Folly's transports all thy mind.

'Mid silken dalliance, mirth, and revel loud,
  Scorning the wisdom learnt in sorrow's school,
Of jesters, parasites, and knaves a crowd
  Usurp thy courts, thy fickle counsels rule,

And bid thee truckle to a tyrant's throne,
  And still while bartering, slave of lawless will,
Thy country's ancient honour and thine own,
  E'en to the brim the cup of rapture fill.

But ah! thy days are numbered : Heav'n has sped
  The fatal shaft that lays thy glory low :
For thee, tho' slumbering 'mid the mighty dead,
  No unbought lay shall rise, nor tear shall flow.

And lo amid the recreant troops that press
  To greet thy brother's kingly step, are seen
The Furies of thine house, with false caress,
  And flatt'ring speech, and meek insidious mien.

And as the serpent's subtle art beguiles
  Th' unwary deer in covert closely laid,
The deadly coil the victim of his wiles
  Enfolds, and piteous moanings fill the glade,

O'er all his pomp a with'ring glance they cast ;
  Its maddening poison rankles in his heart,

His laurels droop as in th' autumnal blast,
The angel guardians of his throne depart.
●

Frantic he riots in misrule, defies
His gathering people, and mistrusts his God,
And long his lineage, tho' his realm he flies,
Shall rue the dire offence and chastening rod.

O'er Scotia's hills brave Nassau's banner waves,
O'er Erin's fens, and Albion's citied plain,
Hushed the wild howl on Aughrim's reeking
graves,
And Boyne no more runs purple to the main.

Yet ere Rebellion folds her crimson'd wings,
Majestically calm, like Rome of old
When Gaul was at her gates, a band of kings,
The patriot senators, their names enrolled

In England's brightest heraldry, debate,
Or by the light illumed of ancient lore
The deep foundations of the shattered state,
Rude structure of their Saxon sires, explore,

Its growing symmetry devoutly scan,
Redeem from slow decay or wasting war,

And mould anew its time-cemented plan,
  Whence Freedom's glorious fabric sprang, from
    far

Dimly by seers descried,—like some vast rock
  That spectral looms beyond the misty sea,
Long looked for refuge from the tempest's shock,
  Achievement of the brave and dwelling of the
    free.

        *   *   *   *   ⸙.

—◆—

VII.

ON LEAVING TALLANTIRE HALL,
CUMBERLAND.

Nov. 1849.

FOUR moons have past since first I heard
Thy timid greeting, gentle bird,
  In sultry noon reposing,
Where girds yon moat thy dwelling rude,
Thine island home, amid thy brood
  In peace maternal dozing.

Ill fares thy shattered tenement
By ruthless sea-gales sorely rent,
   While sweeps the autumnal blast
The sere leaves, where they wove on high
Their ample arching canopy,
   In whirling eddies past.

And like vicissitude thy lot
Hath prov'd, albeit thou know'st it not,
   While on thy sedgy waters,
Or wonted knoll thou sit'st alone
Meekly, like monumental stone,
   Bereft of sons and daughters.

I ask not what their fate hath been,
Since first thou led'st thy nestlings green
   Exulting from the shore,
Full soon, in snow-white plumes array'd,
Awhile in sunshine or in shade
   To sport, and be no more.

I ask not, but thy woes impart
A passing sadness to my heart,
   In sooth unfelt by thee,
While sympathetic bands entwine
My summer's transient joys with thine,
   Who once partook thy glee.

For thine was no unshared domain,
Nor for thy sake alone soft rain
   Distilled, nor suns shone bright,
Nor broad planes spread their tangled shade,
Nor waters welled, nor breezes played,
   Nor streamed the mists of night.

No! there, as on enchanted ground,
Mine imps too joyous pastime found,
   In the insect's glittering wing,
Or opening flow'ret gemmed with dew,
Beholding Heav'n's own magic hue,
   And life's eternal spring.

Light hearts were theirs from morn till eve
To chase the darting fly, or weave
   The daisies' withering wreath,
Or mark their fairy frigate brave
The menace of the mimic wave,
   And toils that lurk'd beneath.

At first, low-cowering in thy nest,
Thou luredst thy nestlings to thy breast,
   Till soon familiar grown,
Thou viewedst with calm unshrinking eye
The giddy rout come rushing by,
   Nor trembledst for thine own.

The past'with thee is gone for ever;
Oblivion's soothing balm can sever
　　The links which nought avail,
Unlike the ties which to his kind
By fears man's heav'n-taught instinct bind,
　　Or hopes that never fail.

Thy joys and griefs alike have fled,
Thou reckest not of thy once lov'd dead,
　　Nor of thy coming doom;
But man recalls, and not in vain,
The number'd hours he meets again
　　Awaking from the tomb.

None miss their reckoning: Time's rude surge
Waves following waves incessant urge,
　　Nor fails the advancing tide,
That wafts, not whelms,—by faith subdued,—
Tho' deep, and turbid, and bestrewed
　　With wreck of human pride;

That wafts, not whelms man's fragile bark,
Tho' darkly loom the past, and dark
　　The stream, till, hush'd its roar,
With present past and future blend, .
A sea of glory without end,
　　When Time shall be no more.

Be our brief portion joy or woe, ᵗ
We may not tarry here below,
  But of Eternity
Frail denizens reclaim the past,
Cling to the present, and forecast
  The future's destiny.

The child, tho' bent on present folly,
No votary crazed of melancholy,
  The past in thought renews,
Or else, in frolic or in tears,
Thro' vistas bright of future years
  Its phantom self pursues.

Or haply if in Life's still eve
To scenes beloved in youth we cleave,
  Where in th' empurpled haze
On groves ancestral, storied streams,
Lone fane, or haunted turret beams
  The light of other days,

Embodying shadows as we roam,
Peopling a visionary home,
  Content the fight to shun,
Voices long silent chide our stay,
And echoes answer, " Come away,
  The triumph is not won."

For sooner in her rifled nest
The bird shall find her wonted rest,
  And heedless bask, the while
From the low beach the tide recedes,
The shoal amid the drifted weeds
  Than shall such dreams beguile.

Chafed by the present's fretting thrall,
Let wealth oppress or pleasure pall,
  Or thwart malignant star
Each high emprize, as faint we cope
With gathering ills, or bravely hope,
  Still gleams the goal from far.

And they who spurn a deathless aim
Can crave proud obsequies, a name
  Upborne on fleeting breath,
And ask,—such vaunts their scoffs belie,—
" O grave, where is thy victory!
  And where thy sting, O death?"

A moment lost to sight, her wave
The sea-bird mounts anew : the grave
  So yields her slain to life.
Grim Death, thy thousand years of sway
To Him are but as yesterday,
  Who bids thee cease from strife.

Prescient while procreant moved sublime
God's Spirit o'er the deep : could Time
 Unfold the vast design,
Or Heav'n's unfathomed mercy span,
His being God forego, or man
 His attributes Divine ?

The hosannahs of Creation's morn
The glory hymn'd of years unborn,
 Redemption's Jubilee ;
The twilight o'er Death's vale that steals
The day-spring from on high reveals,
 As memory's shadows flee.

On the parched heath the blighted flow'r,
That wastes the fragrance of an hour,
 Gives Spring no promise vain,
And what is childhood but the bloom
Of seedling nurtur'd in the tomb ?
 Its incense breathes again.

And as its fount unseen the ray,
So childhood's joys their source betray :
 We bid not reason prove
Truth which the sage may fail to teach,
Nor bard's all-searching vision reach,
 Faith whispers " God is love."

VIII.

ON THE PAPAL AGGRESSION.

1851.

THERE's nothing new beneath the sun,—
In aye-revolving cycle run
Man's hope, and fear, and joy, and sorrow,—
Night's spectres fly the brightening morrow,
Or if Day hide his kingly form,
Brief revel holds the fleeting storm.
Then let Heav'n's blasts their orgies wake,
'Till kings like quiv'ring aspens shake,
And falling stars and heaving ocean
Portend the last foretold commotion,
I'll mount where sounds the din like roar
Of waves on a far distant shore,
And purg'd from earth-born mists my ken,
While to and fro the tribes of men
Are swept as autumn leaves, may scan
Of Providence the unerring plan.

Faith shall arouse my slumb'ring lyre,
And tho' no lofty theme inspire,
Britain, to venturous bard his meed
Vouchsafe, and to my strain give heed.
Nor take, where none is meant, offence,
If allegory veil my sense,
Since forms uncouth may truth convey,
And wisdom prompt a sportive lay,
And prescience, while of legend old
She feigns to speak, her lore unfold.
Then listen, while in homely verse
A tale of Albion I rehearse.

In Westminster's imperial town,
London's twin sister in renown,
Where senates, arbiters of fate,
Decree, while realms the issue wait ;
Where Justice lifts aloft her scales
Unswayed by Faction's fickle gales ;
Where yet unspoiled, a princely dow'r
Gladdens fair Learning's hallowed bow'r ;
Where from the Minster daily rise
Her Church's holy litanies,
And, as to check the suppliant's pride,
Sit Death and Glory side by side,
The votive wreath with cypress twine,
And sceptered pomp in dust enshrine :

City whose generous warmth invites
Guests of all shapes, and tongues, and rites,
While man and beast confiding share
Of equal laws the fostering care,
There dwelt and roam'd, to few unknown,
The native* of another zone.
Her sluggish gait and shaggy vest
Belied the soul that fired her breast,
Nor fang her snout betrayed, nor claw
The terrors of her downy paw.
And as to gaze on mystic might
Unawed instils sublime delight,
When fear scarce felt just crisps the skin,
Nor owns its spell the heart within,
The vilest of the motley rout,
That scann'd the monster round about,
In straining eye and tingling finger
Might feel the fascination linger
That lures th' unwary victim on
'Till, sense enchained, and reason gone,
And flutt'ring pulse, and parting breath,
Confess the wizard grasp of death.

Of foreign guise was he† who led
The brute, while to her solemn tread

---

* Romanism.   † Cardinal Wiseman.

E

A loud tambour responsive drew
The gathering crowd, whose wonder grew
To mark bedizened squires bestride
With courtly air her bushy hide,
Or as she sat on haunch elate,
In mimicry of regal state,
On her behalf obsequious claim
A tribute not of empty fame.

But many a morn's enlivening beam
Had waked the sons of smoke and steam
In square, and street, and alley dense,
Dark haunts of sin and pestilence,
While 'mid the swarming hosts 'twere vain
To seek old Bruin and her train.
Nor sharp alarum, buzz or shout,
Nor shriek, nor rush, nor rabble rout
Told England, as in bygone days,
The bear invok'd the city's gaze.
Meanwhile full soon strange murmurs spread;
'Twas whisper'd she was sick or dead,
Or that infuriate from the bite
Of treacherous foe or rabid spite,
Her guards canine had spurn'd her sway,
And sore beleaguered still she lay.*

---

* Romanism besieged by the French in her own capital.

A pause the onset reinforces,
As sapient Verulam discourses,
And so deemed Bruin, versed as he
In tangled lore of sophistry.
And hark ! ere yet November's sun
Had donned his wintry mantle dun,
The drum's deep tones proclaim again
That Bruin seeks her ancient reign.
Forth from her labyrinth she comes,
Of courts, and alleys, lanes, and slums,*
Where 'neath the Minster's hallow'd shade
In loathsome den her lair is laid,
And where within the Abbey gate,
To lore prebendal dedicate,
And discipline scholastic famed
For many a rebel stripling tamed,†
The close its ample bounds expands,
Erect in regal port she stands.‡
Goodly and gallant is her trim,
With scarlet hose enwrapped each limb,
Her brows with scarlet scull-cap bound :
Around her shoulders deftly wound

---

* So described by Cardinal Wiseman.
† Westminster School.
‡ Cardinal Wiseman issued his first Manifesto from West-
minster.

A Spanish mantle * floats in air,
Her sturdy paws a sceptre bear,
While, robed in scarlet, nimbly wait
Her roguish ministers of state,
And of her princely pedigree
All conscious, and in mimicry
Of arts maternal, frisks behind
A Cub,† the daintiest of his kind.
To celebrate the glorious birth
Old Bruin woos the city's mirth,
And in the fair succession hails
A dynasty that never fails,
'Till bears once more shall rule these nations,
As auspicate twin constellations,
Whose light of old their roamings led
When forests shook beneath their tread,
And shall when Britain's royal dow'r
Melts in the gripe of Ursine pow'r.
Now minstrels chaunt your pæans high,
Let instrumental harmony‡   ·
Blend its loud tones of fife and drum,
Flute or bassoon's soul-stirring hum,

---

* Cardinal Wiseman by birth a Spaniard.
† Anglo-Romanism.
‡ Allusion to the prodigality of instruments, including the
martial fife and drum, employed in the Romish ceremonial.

Or castanets whose merry din
Ushers the festal triumph in,
Where choral bands the dance entwine
Before proud Seville's stateliest shrine.*
O Heav'n, from heathenish rites profane,
From Superstition's gilded chain,
From Spanish arts defend and wiles,
As erst from Spanish might our isles!

And marvell'd much in sooth the crowd,
Now murmuring low, now shouting loud,
As memory, while the descant grew,
Unrolled in dark historic view
The days when Bruin reigned alone,
And brooked no sister near her throne.
Hark! from the Minster sounds the alarm,
Her watchmen† bid her liegemen arm,
Lest rebel rage the shrine invade,
Where meekly sought the Royal maid
In faith the living source whence springs
The might of realms or sway of kings,
All pure from its celestial birth
Untainted by the stains of earth.

---

* Scene actually exhibited at the high altars of the Cathedral of
Seville, and censured at Rome by the Pope.

† The first address in opposition to the Wiseman Manifesto
Proceeded from the Prebendaries of Westminster.

And had not reason's dim eclipse
Thy vision quenched, and sealed thy lips,
Pealed had thy tocsin, nor in vain,
Warden* of yon sepulchral fane,
To whose high charge in custody
Was giv'n of kings and statesmen old,
Sages and priests, and warriors bold,
And bards renown'd the honour'd dust,
A grateful nation's hallow'd trust.

Now parts apace the eager throng,
The gay procession moves along,
And thro' the archway rolls the tide
Of life, and hope, and swelling pride.
The minstrels first in order due
March forth, while banners flaunt the view :
Next Bruin treads with solemn pace,
The Cub her gesture apes with grace,
Her rear the liv'ried lacqueys fence
From insult or impertinence :
The docile dogs come limping after.
Oh ! for an hour of Sidney's† laughter !
No merry limner skill'd as he
To paint such Ursine pageantry.

---

* Dr. Buckland, Dean of Westminster.
† Rev. Sidney Smith.

Oh for thy glance, swift falcon,* keen
As his, which scatheless and unseen
Could pierce like heaven's own bolt its prey.
Say hast thou fled, or shunnest the day
Where moping owlets fold the wing,
And vampires to their victims cling?
Or doth Enchantment's deadly spell
Its willing captive trammel well,
'Till cease to gall the mystic chain?
One swoop had rent its links in twain,
And scatter'd Bruin and her train.†

On sped the tumult, mutters loud
The thunder of the maddening crowd:
Dies on the ear the Minster's chime,
While in its knell all vainly Time
Bids fame from aisles and cloisters grey
Strange welcome to a shroud of clay.
On speeds the tumult, mark ye now
Yon statue: by the lofty brow,

----

* H. B.

† It is worthy of note that Cardinal Wiseman deferred his
Manifesto till just after the death of Sidney Smith and the dis-
appearance of H. B., the two most redoubtable satirists of the
age.   It was surmised that apprehension of collision with the
Romish Hierarchy caused H. B.'s timely retreat.

And eagle glance 'tis his,* the form
Aye seen triumphant in the storm,
Still pointing 'mid the welkin's war
Where faintly glimmer'd Bruin's star.
Long may its light benignant shine
On high-souled Canning's lordly line.

On speeds the tumult ; softly tread,
And chaunt a requiem for the dead,
Ye minstrels, and your uproar cease,
Britons, and bid his spirit peace
Ere yet yon stately hall † be past
Where throbb'd its patriot ardour last :
Spirit of him whose voice of pow'r
Still ruled the tempest's darkest hour,
'Till day, refulgent from the gloom,
Beamed but to gild the victor's tomb.

Nor shun the dark presage awhile
That broods o'er yonder storied pile,‡
Where as a lamb to slaughter led
The martyred sire of monarchs bled,
Who ever blessed the hallowed star
In exile while they roam'd afar ?

---

* Rt. Hon. George Canning, a foremost champion of the political
emancipation of the Roman Catholics.

† House of Sir Robert Peel, another distinguished supporter of
the same cause.   ‡ Whitehall.

The tumult gathers : cease from woe,
And bend your steps in homage low,
Where weaves, unseen by garish day,
Her tangled web imperial sway.*
Grows as it feeds the lust of power ;
So brightens as it bends the flower,
That to the sun its incense brings,
When morning shakes her dewy wings.
Avaunt the spectres wan of death,
Give bold ambition's trumpet breath ;
Time, farewell to thy winters hoary,
Hail summers on a sea of glory.

The minstrels stole a witching measure
From an arch-magician's† treasure,
Of his subtle skill in token,
Who, as Ulster's sage‡ has spoken,
" Whate'er he did in gramarye
Had ever done maliciously,"
Whose spell bade Scotia's wither'd bays
Bloom fresh as in forgotten days,
While yet her mountains stern and wild
Meet pastime found for ursine child,

---

* Downing Street.   † Walter Scott.
‡ Rev. Dr. Cook, of the Presbyterian Synod of Ulster, who
attributed the supposed revival of Popery in Great Britain prin-
cipally to Walter Scott's writings.

Unpruned her spreading forests grow,
Chiefs doff the breech and bend the bow,
With crafty fox for scanty food
To cope once more, or gaunt wolf's brood,
'Till wily Bruin's conquering race
Regain their ancient dwelling place.
'Twas thus the exulting descant rang,
Responsive thus the minstrels sang.

Of all the *culs de sac* so rare,
  Form'd for a statesman's dwelling,
In London far beyond compare,
  Is Downing Street excelling.*

    *   *   *   *   *

---

* " Of all the palaces so fair,
    Formed for a Royal dwelling,
    In Scotland far beyond compare,
    Linlithgow is excelling."—
              Scott's *Marmion.*

Downing Street is roused by the uproar. The officials look awe-struck from the windows. The Premier, Lord John Russell, follows the general impulse. Less moved by the arrogant defiance of Bruin than by the freaks of the Cub reminding him of former vexatious contentions, and perhaps perceiving an opportunity of adding to his stock of political capital, in a luckless hour convulses the nation by his famous Manifesto, called the "Durham Letter."

Pledged to follow its anathemas by legislation, he employs Parliament during an entire session in framing and amending an Act, which fell, as was foreseen, dead from its birth, securing no other purpose than that of a warning against any future attempt to substitute *protests* for *statutes.*

IX.

THE TWO GIANTS,

LEGEND VERSIFIED,* ON THE OCCASION OF THE
ANNUAL MEETING OF THE ARCHÆOLOGICAL
INSTITUTE OF GREAT BRITAIN AND IRELAND,
HELD AT BRISTOL IN 1851.

DEDICATED TO THE PRESIDENT, J. S. HARFORD, ESQ.

OF days renown'd of old I sing,
　When Pen,† thy storied steep
Saw, faithless to her native spring,
　Sweet Avon seek the deep.

---

* The legend runs thus. Two giants, Vincent and Gorham,
contended for the Avon. The former retained possession, while
the latter sought consolation for his defeat in the repose of his
arm-chair, which is still pointed out in the romantic glen of Blaise
Castle, the refreshment of a stream in which he bathed his feet,
and the occasional excitement of an aërial excursion in company
with the Storm King.

† Penpole, a well-known promontory at the junction of the
Avon and Severn.

'Sooth maidens ever love to roam,
  And fragile is the spell
That binds their fickle hearts to home,—
  As roguish bards know well,

And deftly skill'd, when toils enclose
  The unwary victim round,
On Love's light wings to chase the foes,
  And clear th' enchanted ground.

So bright and buoyant, as when first
  She sparkled into life,
Fared Avon forth ; when sudden burst
  The thunder-cloud of strife.

For, as from dark primeval shade
  Emerging, she pursued
Her course, where giants twain survey'd
  The realms their might subdued,

Each from his castle-crag descried
  The nymph with longing eyes,
And emulous with hasty stride
  Rushed forth to grasp the prize.

Groaned Ocean from its depths,—Earth shook,—
  Heaven lowered in storms above,
While from each fierce conflicting look
  Flashed flames of wounded love.

Ye mountains of the Western sun,
  If vocal, as of old,
'Twere yours to tell thro' ether dun
  How rocks in tempest roll'd ;—

Her 'wilder'd waves in dire affright
  How the virgin stream withdrew,
While to the rescue kindly Night
  On ebon pinions flew ;—

And sought each chief his lonesome rest,
  While Avon, far away,
On Severn's softly heaving breast,
  In peaceful slumbers lay.

But soon to greet the victor,—Fame
  Oft wins the coyest fair,—
On Ocean's flood elate she came,
  Where from his rocky lair

Now hoar with years, on tow'r and town,
  On mead or woodland bow'r,
In glory's prime looks Vincent down,
  His bride's imperial dow'r,—

While daily greet his gladden'd view,
  In many a clime unfurled,
The sails that waft her tribute due,
  The trophies of a world.

And passing fair her banks ascend,
  As on her bridal morn :—
Mark when with Spring's bright verdure blend
  Dark yew and whitening thorn

Soft mellowing tints, where beetling brow,
  Knoll or ravine, prolong
Their sinuous course, or valley low,
  Where lingers yet the song

Of gifted bards ; vain Nature's grace
  When Sacrilege, sad sign
Of days degenerate, would efface
  Each lineament Divine.*

Yet limits bound proud Man's control ;
  Despite his boastings vain,
Shall Vincent stand, and Avon roll
  Unfettered to the main.

But luckless Valour claims its bays,
  Where lull'd the mournful wind
The vanquish'd lord of rocky Blaise
  In his moss-grown chair reclin'd.

---

* The rock scenery of the Avon has been much disfigured by
the quarrying.

Soft showers, while rugged Gorham slept,
  Bedew'd his feverish brow,
To cool his limbs the forests wept,
  And streams began to flow.

And foremost from her silvan nook
  Came forth the chief to greet
The naïad of a limpid brook,
  That murmured at his feet.

And destined was that lovely form
  The warrior's soul to cheer,
While vernal airs, or Winter's storm
  Prevail'd, or autumn sere :

But sultry Summer's scorching noon
  Her viewless footsteps fled,
Nor e'en the glimpses of the moon
  Reveal'd her unknown bed.

But now the glen eternal Spring
  Hath clad in living green,
The feather'd warblers fold the wing
  Beneath the forest screen :

And lo—where erst, when the dog-star's beam
  Had pierc'd the shrivelling brake,

Shrank from the wither'd fern the stream,—
The heav'n-reflecting lake.*

Gaunt Gorham, when in musing mood
He woos the bliss of ease,
Deep mirror'd in the unruffled flood
His own grim visage sees :

Or when he soars on the winds away,
By the Storm-King's lures beguiled,
The blackening waves his freaks betray,
And share the frolic wild.

So learn, gay youth, that wedded love,—
Such moral points my tale,—
In pride of pow'r may constant prove,
Or in life's sequester'd vale.

And ye on Durdham's breezy plain
Who brush the morning dew,
Or hail Day's farewell from the main,
Or Gallia's mountains blue ;

And mark that none the soil to till,
Where raged the unearthly fray,
Hath dared, nor mason's puny skill
To shape the mouldering clay ;—

---

* Formed by the late Mr. Harford, who planted the bare part
of the glen with evergreens and other trees.

Save where to guard a hallow'd fount
  Whence Mendip's streams distil,
Upheaves yon solitary mount,*
  Heav'n shield its banks from ill ;—

Rashly deem not 'twas vainly told
  By Heaven's unerring pen
There were giants in the days of old
  To mock the pride of men,

X.

THE ROBIN.

(LANGTON ON SWALE. NOV. 1851.)

As lone I wander'd yestere'en,
  Where sweeps the rushing Swale
By sunny Langton's copse-wood screen
  From Richmond's rocky dale,

Redeeming haply, as I hew'd
  My toilsome path from thrall,
Some sapling monarch of the wood,
  Broad plane, or poplar tall,

* A reservoir for the supply of the town, by water brought from
the Mendip hills, the only encroachment on the Down permitted.

*

I paused where struggled into light
  A holly, to behold
Its glistening leaves and berries bright
  The spiry shrub unfold,

When sudden wing'd his hasty way,
  As mischief to avert,
And perched upon its topmost spray
  A robin plump and pert.

And in his sharp inquiring eye
  And beating breast, methought
I shrewdly guessed the reason why
  My steadfast gaze he sought.

Yes, little bird, I'll spare thy nest;
  Go sing the winter long,
While other warblers seek their rest,
  Thy never-failing song.

Its carols shall my sloth reprove,
  While thro' the circling year
The tribute of thy constant love
  Shall greet thy Maker's ear,

And reason to thine instinct turn,
  In thy rejoicing strain
Love that may gladden bliss to learn,
  Or soothe the pang of pain.

XI.

STANZAS

ADDRESSED TO A FRIEND WHO HAD ADOPTED THE
METRE IN WHICH THEY ARE WRITTEN IN A
VOLUME OF POEMS JUST PUBLISHED.

Nov., 1853.

I SPORT with my rhymes
As a cat at times
With a mouse whom she holds by invisible chain;
Tho' he scamper away,
Her destined prey,
He must rue the sure gripe of her clutches again :

Or like some poor fool
Of a stripling at school,
Who breaks in a fit of vagary his bounds,
Where'er he may roam
He must needs come home,
Like a knave dogg'd by bailiffs or quarry by hounds :

Or like truant ship,
That seems to slip
From her moorings aloof from the wave-beaten
    shore,
Tho' she drift on the tide,
'Tis but to abide
On her shadow as stiff and as still as before :

Or as planet forth cast,
In his orbit vast
To revolve, and revolving for ever to run ;
Tho' he fain would war
With each distant star,
He must bide as he circles the course of the sun.

How blest he who hears
The music of spheres,
To haunt with the blind bard its sources sublime,
Whose ears no more tingle
With the ne'er-failing jingle,
Which mocks as it woos the sad echoes of time.

.

XII.

IMPROMPTU AT LANGTON.

1854.

WHY am I thus bereft and lone,
Where are my joyous children gone ?
Oh may no ill their paths betide,
O God their steps in mercy guide !
Beneath thy sheltering wings, O take
And shield them for a Saviour's sake !
A Father's blessing on them rest,
Yea, bless them, and they shall be blest !

———◆———

XIII.

THE DRAKES OF KIPLIN.

ON SEEING A FLOCK OF THESE UNMATED BIRDS ON
THE WATER OF KIPLIN HALL, THE RESIDENCE
OF THE COUNTESS OF TYRCONNEL.*

.

1856.

OF all the fledg'd sages of brooks, rivers, lakes,
Or of fens, wolds, or surf-beaten shore,

---

* Now the property of the Hon. Captain Carpenter, R.N.

None have prattled so well as the brave Kiplin
    drakes
    Since the days of good Æsop of yore.

Then hark to their strains which could silence the
    song
    Of the bird in the brake and the frog in the pool,
While Swale thro' his withies crept slowly along,
    As when ice-bound he lists to the carols of Yule.

Hark, hark! tho' the old Attic warblers are still
    And the sweet swans of Mincio their death-notes
      have sung,
Other web-footed minstrels are tuning the bill ;
    Hark, hark! did such wisdom e'er flow from
      the tongue ?
      *   *   *   *   *

" Quack, quack! let the mad world go round,
    What boots it to us drakes of Kiplin,
As we bask on the bank, or the waves as we
    bound
    In the wake of our gambols are rippling ?

Quack, quack! let them wed as they please,
    To their mates of like feather a cooing,
Catch the Kiplin drakes at such freaks as these,
    Old Charon shall first go a wooing.

Quack, quack! let them boast of their broods,
  The nursing old fools and their prattle,
Enough for us drakes is the mirth of our floods,
  And the wild stormy winds as they rattle.

Quack, quack! when the winter sets in,
  Let them go where they will with the swallow:.
Oh joy to be rid of their horrible din,
  We drakes are too knowing to follow.

Quack, quack! in vain do ye cozen,
  Sleek ducks of dark Hornby's still waters :*
We guess the grim Duke can wring necks by the
    dozen,
  Away with you, ye and your daughters.

Quack, quack! 'spite the long-snouted ranger,
  Whom Milbank's rout† ne'er could o'ertake,
We'll gallantly roam as we list, fear of danger
  Ne'er ruffles the plume of a drake.

Quack, quack! tho' from soft downy slumbers
  We wake to miss one or another ;
Avails it to us, since we reck not of numbers,
  To rue the queer fate of a brother ?

---

* The late Duke of Leeds had a decoy on a small lake at Hornby
Castle, and was expert as executioner.
  † The hounds of Mr. Mark Milbank, of Thorp Perrow.

Quack, quack ! let the cook's grisly fingers
 For the prize with sly Reynard contend,
Be ours without stint life's delight while it lingers,
 No matter how soon it may end."

   * * * * *

Now skill'd in the maxims of life's narrow span,
 Proud Stoic and Libertine tippling,
Say whence the rude wisdom untutor'd by man
 Of the jolly old Drakes of Kiplin ?

" Quack, quack !" to your nostrums is all their reply,
 Dull grey-beard and addle-brained stripling,
" In the mirth of our sires as we've lived we will
 die,"
Quoth the jolly old drakes of Kiplin.

XIV.

ON VISITING THE RUINS OF HEIDELBERG BY MOON-
LIGHT, OCT. 2, 1857, IN COMPANY WITH THE
HON. C. J. SHORE.

SILENT we gazed ; the scene was passing fair ;—
No other eye save the full-orbed moon's was there,
As o'er the woodland she looked coldly down
On Neckar's stream, and vine-clad hills, and old
 imperial town.

Yet Heidelberg, thy hills of laughing vine,
Thy wide champaign, and Neckar's silvery line,
Or lost or glimmering in the dim expanse,
In vain beguil'd us where we stood in speechless
    trance.

Above, the star-lit canopy of heav'n,—
Beneath the mould'ring pavement,—round us riv'n,
Tottering or fall'n, yet beauteous in decay,
And glorious as in its prime the Castle's ruins
    grey.

O'er arch and portal, niche and pediment,
Terrace and tow'r, with shade inwoven blent
Of foliage dank, the mellowing lustre gleamed ;
Like some bright vision of the past the gorgeous
    fabric seemed,

Yet of the past forsaken.   Backward roll
Ye ages, and reveal historic scroll,
And quaint heraldic banner tales of death :—
Avails the unknown dead the clarion's thrilling
    breath,

Low chant or lofty pæan ?   On the hill
Mute were the echoes, and the grove was still,
And from the roofless hall the bird of night
As weary of her watch had wing'd her sullen
    flight,

While hush'd the winds, whose moan when leaves
    are sere
Hath hymned the dirge of the departing year,
And 'mid its orisons the night dews wept,
Oft since yon crumbling tow'rs destruction's besom
    swept.

A birthright dire the death-feud of our race
Hath proved since proud man marr'd Creation's
    face.
Type of his fall, majestic tho' of pow'r
Bereft, as still were thine for aye imperial dow'r,

Fortress, thou frownest o'er battle-fields, whose
    slain
Sought thee a fated guerdon, but in vain,
Victors and vanquished phantoms of a dream;—
Where glared the fitful pageant, sleeps the still
    moonbeam.

Where rest the brave, or wastes the storied pile
When cheers the day's bright ray we pause
    awhile,
But when the moonlit sward we softly tread
We linger as we muse and commune with the
    dead.

They come,—no gibbering denizens of night
Lured by the glimpses of Heav'n's mystic light,—
With converse high to nerve us for the strife,
That waits us ere as they we quit this coil of life.

Nor fade those moonlit tow'rs from memory's view
Like some false mirage of.the melting dew:
We marvel and are gone, but of an hour
May own till life's last throb the heav'n-appointed
    pow'r.

And at night's solemn noon, when slumbers fail,
I'll to thy silent courts, o'er Neckar's vale
Where ruled the Palatine, in thought repair,
Like some unbodied sprite who once had dwelling
    there.

Time-worn, and scathed by storm and strife, as
    one
Whose work in other days was nobly done,
Thou for thyself hast earn'd from friends and foes
Respite from lawless rage, a sanctuary of repose;

Whose bounds no spoiler's hands save Time's
    shall dare
Assail, a rock which Time's rude flood shall spare,
While round thee, citadel of ages, rave
The warring winds in vain, and wreck-engulfing
    wave.

Peace in whose bosom stirring memories dwell,
Not death-like as the stillness of the cell,
Is thine: to such the storm-tost spirit clings
As to her ark the dove, and plumes her weary
    wings. .

By distance temper'd soothes the din of life,
With music sweet the tempest's moan is rife,
Or the vex'd ocean's melancholy roar,
While in some rock-bound bay our shatter'd bark
    we moor;

Nor less Time's far spent echoes, tho' to rest
They woo not, nor may stay Heav'n's bidden
    guest:
The stranded wrecks that in the surf decay
The seaman mourns aloof and plies his homeward
    way.

Vainly our tribute on the cairn we cast,
Or weep in dreams a visionary past,
Or with the patriot sigh, or pensive swain
O'er nation's passing prime, or elegy's sad strain.

Bury the dead their dead : to nobler strife
Than tasks oblivion's worm awakes the life
Redeemed of glorious spirits as they throng
To swell the pomp and prove the high behest of
    song.

And Heidelberg, albeit thine harp unstrung
The wild wind sweep, yet Poesy is young,
As when up Pindus' steep she led the Nine,
Or "lured to brighter worlds" the prophet bard
 divine :

Or when thine ancient lays, in hall or bow'r,
Beguiled the lone or cheered the festal hour,
Lays of the Niebelungen loved of old
In convent, court, and camp, and many a mountain
 hold :

Where'er ice-cradled rivers wound their way
Thro' reedy swamps, or forests 'reft of day,
Wilds of the brindled boar, or antlered stag,
Or where o'er terraced vineyards towered the
 castled crag.

Or as when, 'mid rude warfare's ceaseless clang,
To robber-chiefs thy wand'ring minstrels sang
Of love and chivalry and valour mild,
And Christ's own Church that shrove her own
 repentant child ;

Of sorceries dire, and beauty's gentle spell,
And visions bright that beam'd on sainted cell,
And cloister'd charity, whose open door
Welcom'd the pilgrim lorn, nor spurned the sup-
 pliant poor.

Yet Heidelberg, of steel-clad chieftains queen,
And mitred lords, thine ancient tow'rs have seen,—
What time dread Cluny's seer the doom foretold,—
What tyrants scourged the realm and wolves
     devoured the fold;

'Till rose the champion of the Crucified :
Ill a monk's cowl his fiery soul belied,
Foremost in thought or act the rage to dare
Of sceptered priests, and fiends of Hell and upper
     air.

And Poesy had marked him for her own,
Ere yet the Church his erring zeal had known,
Or heav'n-taught truth inspired, in forest deep,
Or star-lit cell, while wont his vigils lone to keep.

And while by faith he foiled the Tempter's pow'r,
Or veil'd in light, or in the darker hour,
His rugged native speech he tuned to praise :
Nor loves his Fatherland alone his hallow'd lays :

O'er Swedish Vasa's dust, at evensong,
I've heard Upsala's snow-girt aisles prolong,*
And bannered hosts, as erst on Lutzen's plain,
O'er far Sclavonia waft the old triumphant strain;

---

* The occasion alluded to was the celebration (1831) in Upsala
Cathedral of the 1000th anniversary of the introduction of Chris-
tianity, and of the 300th of that of the Reformation, into Sweden.

Triumphant: yet what ceaseless wail of woe
For thrice ten years proclaimed, while, foe to foe,
Brothers, and sires, and sons embattled stood,
The faith triumphant still, albeit baptized in blood.

Thus nations learn to suffer and to shun,
And sons to achieve the work their sires begun,
Since bright examples to all times belong,
And but to warn and prove hath Heav'n allow'd
　　the wrong.

Else vain the Swede's emprize, the spirit calm,
The hero's falchion and the martyr's palm,
And Heav'n to vain remorse his foeman doomed,
As on his quailing glance the rifled city loomed.

Else, why to Poesy to shape the unknown,
Shadowed by myth, or symbolized by stone,
The subtle skill, the holy mission given,
To trace on shifting sands the footprints sure of
　　heav'n,

In no part of that kingdom was the ceremonial more solemnly
observed than in the Metropolitan Church, under the auspices of
the Archbishop. Most imposing was the effect of the singing
Luther's Hymn by the congregation, consisting of 4000 persons,
as the light streamed over the building from the brilliantly illu-
minated tomb of Gustavus Vasa.

As on the pathless deep or viewless wind ?
Or whence the light in deathless song enshrined,
That beams on the rough path her sons have trod,
And leads, or fain would lead, their pilgrim steps
    to God :

Light of the life in Bürger's pulse could thrill,
Or in brave Körner's death notes linger still,
Or gentle Schiller's sweet-toned strains inspire,
Or the wild wayward might of Goethe's wizard
    lyre ?

Light that, where howls thro' old Iona's fane
The blast, or sweeps the Marathonian plain,
No earthly flame, shall unextinguished burn,
Where saints or heroes strove, to live or die we
    learn :

Or glimmers yet in Melrose' moonlit aisle,
Tho' knavish gramarye no more beguile,
And Dryburgh's shades the minstrel's dust embower
Who wove each wonderous spell, Magician of his
    hour ?

And German Poesy, long wont to roam,
Hath found once more beneath thy skies a home.
Renown'd in story flow to song unknown
Thy Danube forest-girt, or arrowy Rhone,

Or "wide and winding Rhine?" By Iser's wave
Chaunts not the bard the requiem of the brave?
Are mute in Weimar's halls the strains for ear
Of seraph meet or fiend, which monarchs loved to
    hear?

Delights thee Freedom? seek the land of Tell:
Or Power? its path the wolf hath tracked full well
From Hapsburg's keep, or Hohenzollern's height,
Where Prussia's eagle fledged his pinion for his
    flight,

Or where grim Wallenstein a world defied:
Or patriot ardour? Lo where drooped the pride
Of conqu'ring Gaul, or waned on Adria's flood
The crescent, while thy youth the Moslem's might
    withstood:

Or guileless faith? go mourn the hapless maid
Victim of hellish arts, or, where betrayed,
A living corse amid the wondering dead,
His long repining love the spectre horseman led.

And guards yon towers no visionary band?
Vandal, withhold thy sacrilegious hand,
Nor tempt the wrath of liegemen skill'd a shield
Of pure ethereal mould and sword of flame to
    wield.

Now farewell Heidelberg, once more farewell ;
Of joys and sorrows past those accents tell,
For I have trod thy grass-grown courts before,
And those who sought my side shall tread those
    courts no more.

Yes, twice ten years twice told have winged their
    flight
Since here I mused with one* in young delight,
With whom in cloistered walk or linden bower
By Granta's silent stream I shared the studious
    hour,

Or breasted Alpine height, or met the day
On old lagune, or legendary bay,
Of art revived surveyed the halcyon reign,
Or dreamed of ancient Greece on Pœstum's
    pillared plain.

Friend of my youth, when age had snowed his
    brow,
Near Granta's silent stream we laid him low,
Beside the fane his pious skill had reared,
Amid the weeping flock his sainted presence
    cheered :

---

* The late Rev. Harvey James Sperling, of Lattenbury Hill,
Rector of Papworth St. Agnes, in Huntingdonshire.

Heir of the fair demesne that spread around,
In him lord, pastor, father, friend they found ;
While from his lips and life persuasion flowed,
And in his daily walk they marked their heaven-
ward road.

A sister, too, now numbered with the blest,
With me those towers, that bode not lasting rest,
Beheld in youthful bloom.   Ah ! with my line
A tributary wreath let fond remembrance twine.

———◆———

XIV.

THE LITTLE BOMBARDIER.

On the 30th July, 1860, the Bristol Volunteer Artillery practised
firing from a couple of 18 pounders at a mark placed in the Severn
opposite the mouth of the Avon, causing no slight alarm to the
juvenile portion of the spectators.

NAPOLEON calls the world to arms :
   To a martial strain give ear :
I sing of war and its alarms,
   And of a little Bombardier.

'Twas a rampart rude on a grass-grown beach ;
   Hard by the pilots' steer
Where guards yon phare the narrowing reach :
   The little Bombardier ;

G 2

Bristowe's famed channel, whence of old
  On either hemisphere
Her argosies pour'd forth her gold :
  The little Bombardier ;

And princely Canynge launch'd his fleet,
  A Churchman skill'd to rear
A shrine for the Holy Virgin* meet :
  The little Bombardier.

On Portice-head a storm cloud lowered,
  And Cambria's mountains drear,
On Pen's sweet uplands half-embowered,
  The little Bombardier ;

And slumbering Avon's bed of mud,
  And not a ray to cheer
The dismal isle, the doleful flood :
  The little Bombardier :

Where once the caitiff's pennon hung,
  Who slew Sir John Goodyear,
And where his limbs all blackening swung † :
  The little Bombardier.

---

* Church of St. Mary Redcliff.

+ The ship's officer employed by Captain Goodyear, R.N., to strangle his brother, Sir John, whom the Captain and some of his crew had in broad day dragged from a house in College Green,

The guns are primed and shotted too,
    And brave the martial gear
Of gunners clad in red and blue :
    The little Bombardier.

Now marksman, steady be thine aim,
    Remember, Volunteer,   ·
The guerdon of thy skill is fame :
    The little Bombardier.

Bang, bang, whiz, whiz, see, see the splash !
    Alas ! what do we here ?
Oh dear ! how could we be so rash ?
    The little Bombardier.

Stop, stop your ears, and close your eyes,
    The children die of fear ;
Papa can't hear their piercing cries :
    The little Bombardier.

Harness the horse : he'll restive prove,
    We'll walk then to the rear :
What perils wait on those we love !
    The little Bombardier.

Bristol to a boat in the Avon, and conveyed on board his frigate
anchored at the mouth of the river.   He and his principal paid the
penalty of their crime at Bristol, and his bones hung for about a
century in chains on the above-mentioned island appropriated to
such purposes.   The " State Trials " contain a full account of this
horrible affair.

All safe, the driver mounts his box :
"The way, ye gentles, clear."
Vanish the river, isle, and rocks :
The little Bombardier.

Turns out, as on a gala day,
The merry town of Shire—
Hampton, for who would not be gay
For the little Bombardier ?

Steeds in King's Weston Park are prancing,
And troops of children dear,
And men and maids are deftly dancing :
The little Bombardier ?

And cricket wakes the drowsy down :
Bring lots of bread and beer,
And greet with chimes old Bristowe town :
The little Bombardier.

Long live the Major to command,
And every staunch compeer,
To shield from harm our glorious land,
And the little Bombardier :

And our striplings bold, and the heir of Stoke,
And recruits of many a year,
To slay a foe, or crack a joke
With the little Bombardier.

And drink, when he is stiff and cold,
To the memory of the Seer,
Who your luck foretold, while he sang of old
Of the little Bombardier.

And welcome any of his line
To Bristowe's loyal cheer,
And the minstrel's wreath shall deck the shrine
Of the little Bombardier.

XVI.

THE CENTENARY OF THE BELL.

LANGTON.—1861.

THE peaceful Sabbath's noon had past,
And the dim sunbeam faded fast
  Of a mid-winter's day,
Where, toiling through a waste of snow,
Dark Swale was scarcely seen to flow
  In the gloomy twilight grey.

And as to bless the hallowed flood,
Memorial of twin martyrs' blood,
  Stood Langton's lonely fane;
While heaved around the sacred sod,
As when its mounds the Saxon trod,
  And the Norman, and the Dane.

By twice four hundred summers seared,
And scathing winters' frosts hath reared
  Its arch yon portal quaint ;
Nor vainly are the walls bedeck'd
By skill of earlier architect,
  And zeal of elder Saint.

And as of old from bended knee
Now rose the solemn litany
  Of priest and people there ;
While saddened was the suppliant throng,
As blended with the evensong
  A brief but heartfelt pray'r.

It asked of heav'n a child's sweet life,
Few words and faint, while spoke the strife
  Of faith with boding fear,
Deep utterance of a parent's soul
And of the church's love, while stole
  Down many a cheek the fear.

The vacant seat betokened well,
The sick one claimed as by a spell
  Her mother's joyless smile ;
The sisters twain sat side by side,
Methought the third might ne'er abide
  Within that holy aisle.

And as our homeward steps we wound
Where by the snowdrift's pall fast bound
  The lowly tombstones lay,
Methought ere on our path again
A Sabbath dawned, a funeral train
  Might blacken all the way.

And as with anguish from the grave
We turned to Him who died to save,
  He seem'd to seek His own,
A seraph purged from soil of earth
To hymn redeemed her second birth
  With angels round the throne.

But ere the hours on hastening wing
Welcomed that Sabbath morn, while Spring
  Had doffed her wintry shroud,
And wreathed her brow each early flower,
And vocal at her call were bower,
  And brake and fleecy cloud,

Hope smiled again where the sick child lay,
And on the eve of the holy day
  Around was heard the din
Of gathering footsteps, voices rife,
And revelry of healthful life,
  And festal cheer within.

And down th' accustomed alley green,
The churchway path, ere noon were seen,
  Fliing in order due,
Fair village maidens side by side,
A bridegroom and his destined bride,
  And friends and kindred few.

The warbling woods gave merry cheer,
And the voice of the bell was sharp and clear,
  As rose the white-robed priest ;
And the sisters sat where they sat before,
But none the garb of mourning wore,
  For the sound of woe had ceased.

While a bashful pair stood hand in hand,
And the priest he knit the holy band,
  And spirits were light and free,
For the prayer had been heard of many a heart,
And the angel of death had stayed his dart,
  And welcome the bridal glee.

And thou fulfill'st thy mission well,
'Twixt earth and heav'n, time-hallowed bell,
  Thy fitting dwelling place ;
Where thou thine hundred years hast swung,
And spoken, tho' with speechless tongue,
  To man's unheeding race.

At morn, at noon, at dead of night
We've heard thee chide the lingering light,
  Startle the lab'ring swain,
Or from thy windy watch-tower scare
The owlet that had nestled there
  As in death's unvexed domain.

Man would forecast his destiny :
Sworn herald of eternity,
  Thou own'st not his control :
Be joy or grief our portion giv'n,
It comes in its own time from heav'n
  Thy message to the soul.

To universal man addrest,
An echo finds in every breast
  The greeting of our doom ;
Now soft as April's balmy shower,
Now rude as blast that rends the tower,
  Or trump that bursts the tomb.

The infant born in Christ anew,
And " glistening with baptismal dew,"
  Unconscious hears thy call,
Which bids him, liegeman of the Cross,
Anon by gain-transcending loss,
  And freedom's welcome thrall,

By links of love we may not sever,
Which, heav'n-wrought, bind true souls for ever
    Tho' dust to dust return ;
By tears which hopeful mourners shed,
And requiem of the sainted dead
    The victor's crown to earn.

Our mutual woe and weal we share,
As thy deep death-notes ask our prayer,
    Or chimes their vigils keep ;
We hear in thine the Church's voice,
And in the general joy rejoice,
    Or weep with those that weep.

Then ask not why that knell, where lowers
A death-cloud on yon city's towers,
    Thus early sounds and late ;
While awestruck peasants shrink aloof,
And scarce the clang of car or hoof
    Is heard within her gate.*

And silent is her once-thronged mart,
And stand her denizens apart
    Whispering of peril near,

---

* The incidents alluded to in this and the following stanzas
are chiefly supplied by the author's recollection of two visits to
Dumfries during the dreadful cholera of 1833.

Or wildly hurry to and fro
To soothe or fly the general woe,
  Like panic-stricken deer.

And marks the lifted sash where lies
The corse unwatched, while streaming eyes
  And wringing hands betray
The kindred in the desert street,
The glance that strains yet fears to meet
  The death cart on its way.

A moment on the silence steals
The rumbling of the dreaded wheels,
  A moment and 'tis past ;
And the ceaseless bell's deep undertone
Blends with loud sob or stifled groan,
  Like the sough of the fitful blast.

And sadly up the church crowned brow
And thro' the graveyard's portal slow
  The marshalled mourners file,
While grows beneath their faltering tread
Of the garnered harvest of the dead,
  The still increasing pile.

Nor deem it strange the knell, that tolls
The farewell of departed souls
  And doom of breathless clay,

Hath power to purge the spell-bound air
From noxious taint and e'en to scare
   The foul fiend from his prey.

While prayer unbidden, as from dale
And hill ascends the voice of wail,
   Owns in His wrath the king
Of terrors as affrighted cower
The tenants of the leafy bower,
   When the falcon's on the wing.

The ocean's roar, and thunder's peal,
And earthquake's throes Heav'n's voice reveal;
   And pestilence, O bell,
Tho' mute and stealthy in its round,
Utterance no less Divine hath found
   In thy soul-piercing knell.

Nor vainly to the Atlantic surge
Responsive rose a nation's dirge,
   When autumn's leaf was sere,
And the tocsin the dread silence broke,
As if avenging angel spoke
   To Albion's startled ear.

And wept in low or lordly home,
As swift-winged from the minster's dome
   Woe on its errand sped,

Peasant and prince as in that night
When Egypt, smitten in her might,
　Bewailed her first-born dead.

Of ancient kings first-born and heir,
We mourned thy blighted bridal fair,
　And infant's early doom,
While in community of grief,
We sought from dark despair relief,
　As we laid thee in the tomb;

And in the knell that bade us share
Imperial grief, His call to prayer
　We heard who paid the price　.
Of man's redemption, could atone
For guilt's inheritance, and own
　A nation's sacrifice.

For scarce of winters twain the snows　.
Had blanched the field of vanquish'd foes
　When Albion led the war:
Nor sign presaged, nor seer descried
The passing cloud awhile should hide
　Her destiny's bright star.

None recked in fight or festal hour
Of bride discrowned or forfeit dower,
　When Gaul's proud eagles fled,

While blood-begrimed stood victory,
Where bleached beneath th' inclement sky
  Her yet unburied dead.

And who may tell, to battle clang
While peal on peal responsive rang,
  If Albion homage due
Withheld from Him our hearts who steeled,
And to our foes the doom revealed
  Of fated Waterloo?

Let kings a nation's tribute claim;
Tower'd cities sound the trump of fame
  And loud hosannahs raise:
The lowly hamlet's simple tale,
Annals of Life's sequestered vale
  Thy call to pray'r and praise

No less, thou ancient bell, shall task,
As thy solemn soothing strain we ask
  Or spirit-stirring chime,
Our sires' loved birthright, boon of Heav'n,
To hallow the brief sorrows given,
  Or fleeting joys of Time.

A hundred years—a fitful dream,
Thy past 'tis gone like yon swift stream
  While yet it murmurs by;

But still we mourn not while thy voice
Bids us amid our tears rejoice,
   Type of Eternity.

A hundred years to come, the morn
Of generations yet unborn,
   And still with man may'st thou,
While 'neath the monumental stone
We sleep forgotten and unknown,
   Plead prophet-tongued as now.

And tho' sweet bell,* thy natal hour
When pealed the minster's stately tower,
   None deemed thy hollow span,
Boast of the Northern craftsman's skill,
Responsive to the trump might thrill,
   That speaks the doom of man,

Haply, when vanish as a scroll
The heavens, and each unbodied soul
   Reclaims its mouldering clay,
Triumphant with night's last farewell,
The death tones of thy parting knell
   May herald endless day.

---

* Wrought at York by a celebrated bell-founder.

XVII.

THE BELLS OF OUSELEY.

1864.

On a charming spot on the right bank of the Thames, between Runnymede close on one side, and Windsor on the other, stands a much frequented public-house, bearing the sign of " The Bells of Ouseley." It is said to be of high antiquity. A friend of mine, an old inhabitant of Windsor, informed me that he believed there was a legend respecting the Bells, but he was unable to discover it. A visit to the place in June, 1864, suggested the following lines.

From sunny meads where alders quiver,
 From groves of stately lime,
Ouseley's bells, where winds yon river,
 What means your ceaseless chime ?

Though light as wanton summer cloud,
 Or bubble of the stream,
That mirrors every hue, the crowd
 May spurn the poet's dream,

Mystic strains, o'er lea forsaken
 While steal the shades of night,

Memories as of yore awaken
Of unalloyed delight :

As when dawned the festal morning,
Such carols long ago
Rousing at the cock's shrill warning
The slumbering world below.*

When sire and stripling, man and maid,
In gallant trim would meet,
Where Mammon all his wealth displayed
Adown the well-thronged street :

In steel resplendent kings beprankt,
And queens in furbished gold ;
Bedizened maidens quaintly ranked
With red-cross warriors bold :

By halberd marked, and mace and chain,
Our city's lordly mayor,
And Noah and his motley train,
All mated pair and pair :

While soared on painted wings aloft
Ambition to the skies,
Or taught the breeze her skiff to waft
On far and free emprize ;

---

* Early Surrey recollections of an annual visit to the celebrated Croydon Fair.

Or urged in ever-circling maze
　The flying courser's speed,
While sly old Punch allured to ways
　That to the gallows lead ;

And jubilant her steadfast voice
　The Church raised o'er the din,
Bidding the revellers who rejoice,
　Rejoicing cease from sin.

Scarce heard, when thrills on high the lark,
　Of bygone years the chime
Renews, as evening shades grow dark,
　The fading hues of time.

Hills, where my truant boyhood roved,
　Far o'er yon woodland rear
Their fir-crown'd heights : the fields beloved,
　I hail, the lonely meer,

And mazy streams, 'mid warbling bowers
　That wander at their will,
Where beams on ever-blooming flowers
　A living lustre still ;

No more bedimmed by mists of earth,
　Nor veiled by nightly gloom,
For the " dewy " radiance " of its birth
　Is of the morning's womb."

Sweet as at night's still noon to seer,
  When weave the stars their spells,
The mystic music of the sphere,
  Your chime, unearthly bells.

Such the greeting I remember,
  And the hour was bright and calm,
Tho' the winds of drear December
  Chaunted their mournful psalm,

And old Skiddaw's head was hoary,
  As cloud begirt he frowned
From his pinnacle of glory
  On lone sepulchral ground,

On a wedded pair attended
  By a young and fair array,
Some o'er whose dust we since have bended
  And others far away ;

While death's sad emblems seemed to chide
  Gay mirth and revel loud,   .
And bid of nuptial veil the bride
  More fitly don the shroud.

But hallow'd are the links that bound us
  In freer realms above,
Nor less the pledges that surround us
  Of never dying love ;

Of the Church's festal union,
  And of each white robed guest,
Bridal banquet, and communion
  Of happy saints at rest.

Yon bells, or does illusion vain
  My dreaming sense beguile ?
I hear your old historic strain,
  Your proud heroic chime !

E'en as in Albion's halcyon hour,
  When throned in might serene
From booming fort and pealing tower
  She welcom'd forth her Queen,

Scion of stalwart kings of old,
  Weird lords of sea and plain,
Whose shadowy forms time's mists unfold,
  To her ancestral fane ;

Fane renowned of martial story,
  Revered of sainted life,
Proud sepulchral home of glory
  And goal of kingly strife ;

Of such as nobly wrought and bled,
  Or wooed or won the gem
That sparkles on her youthful head,
  Her triune diadem.

Yet no boding note of sorrow
Blent sadly with the acclaim
Heralding a brightening morrow
Of aye enduring fame :

While the Church spake long and loudly
From twice ten thousand towers :
" Maiden monarch deal not proudly
In this free land of ours :

" On, though rough the path of duty,
To the victor's bright abode ;
Tarry not though health and beauty
May fail thee on the road.

" Brave deeds beseem thy lineage high :
Not cradled the renown
Of thine emblazoned ancestors
In sea-girt tower and town,

" But where lingers, mid the waving
Of legend-haunted woods,
Deathless fame, and 'mid the raving
Of Boreal winds and floods :

" E'en where flagged Rome's ample pinion,
And still th' unsetting sun
From the Pagan's dark dominion
Beheld fresh trophies won.

" Fair monarch, by th' eternal word
    That wielded in the fight
Heroic Alfred's heav'n-wrought sword,
    And holy Edward's might :

" By the barons sworn of Runnymede
    When Freedom held the pen,
(Nor deem where whispers now the reed
    Yon bells were silent then) ;

" By the warriors mailed of Palestine,
    And lowlier men of heart
Who disenthralled our captive shrine,
    Nor shunned the martyrs' part ;

" And by the dungeon, chain, and stake,
    And by the torturing flame,
For Christ's and for thy people's sake
    Abide thou still the same."

Yet none could reck of trouble near,
    Nor seer the doom portend,
How in the winter of the year,
    Ye bells, your chime should blend

With Nature's sympathetic groan,
    As hymned the doleful blast,
And the swoll'n river's sullen moan
    The dirge of glory past,

Responsive to the cannon's boom,
And minster's deep-toned knell,
As widowed to the silent tomb
A monarch bade farewell.

And weeps mute grief in Windsor's halls
Disconsolate her prince,
Nor clarion of her stately walls
Hath waked the echoes since.*

When cheers not hope the vale of sorrow
The gloom what phantoms haunt !
But dawns on darkest night a morrow :
Ye grisly troops avaunt !

And by thine oath, fair mourner, sworn
At famed St. Peter's shrine,
Thy marriage vows, and pledges borne
To Britain's royal line,

Thy wedded troth's unsullied light,
And lustre of his life,
Thy guide, liege Consort, stainless knight
And shield in toil and strife ;

* June, 1864.

And by His patience, Man of Woes,
  Whose sufferings purged our dross,
And by His might who wrung from foes
  The triumph of His Cross,

Come forth as brightening from the gloom
  The peerless star of eve,
Nor let the chill damp of the tomb
  To lofty purpose cleave ;

Skilled in the chastened, hallowed lore
  'Tis giv'n to grief to attain :
So dim eclipse shall veil no more
  The glory of thy reign.

Ouseley's bells in joy and gladness
  Still welcome be your chime,
Tho' scoffers hold our dreaming madness
  As in the olden time.

Life has its dreams : in dreams may we
  Our pastime find as they,
And snatch from myth's dark mystery
  The moral of a lay.

XVIII.

ON SEEING A SILVER SALVER,

WHICH HAD BEEN PRESENTED TO SIR ROBERT H.
INGLIS BY THE GRILLON CLUB, AND BY HIM
BEQUEATHED TO SIR THOMAS D. ACLAND, HANDED
ROUND THE DINNER TABLE WELL LADEN WITH
CONSTANTIA, AT KILLERTON, NOV. 16TH, 1864.

CONVIVIAL Inglis, on his salver bright
The old Constantia gives its tint aright,
Type of his spirit, genial, sweet, and strong,
And generous as the juice that tasks my song ;
And potent, too, to temper or inspire
The Christian's ardour and the patriot's fire,
" The feast of reason and the flow of soul."
Fill, Grillon's brothers, high the sparkling bowl
In saddened silence to his memory.
None braver, better, and more loved than he,
None readier at his country's call to dare,
Or at the board your social glee to share :

Staunch statesman, steadfast friend, companion
    boon,
By God and man approved, ah! snatched from
    earth too soon!

———◆———

XIX.

ON SEEING A BRIGHT RAY SETTLE ON THE FORE-
HEAD OF CHANTREY'S DEAD INFANT, AT KILLER-
TON, SIR T. D. ACLAND'S. NOV. 16TH, 1864.

THE sun set fair on Killerton,
And on a niche full brightly shone
That sepulchred a sleeping one,
Relic of sorrows past and gone.
And seemed the brow it fell upon
To quicken, and the breathing stone
To utter, not the dying groan,
But the song of one before the throne,
Hymning His praise who died to atone
For such, and living claims His own!
The sculptor's skill will heav'n disown?
Ask of the parent's heart, for such its pow'r hath
    known.

XX.

1. The character you most admire in history.
2. Your favourite character in fiction.
3. The character you most dislike in History.
4. The character you most dislike in fiction.
5. Your favourite author.
6. Your favourite flower.
7. Your favourite poet.
8. Your favourite composer
9. Your favourite name.
10. Your favourite artist.
11. Your favourite occupation.
12. The one you most dislike.
13. Your favourite dainty.
14. The virtue I most love.
15. The vice I most dislike.
16. Your favourite motto.
17. Your favourite pastime.
18. Your favourite fruit.
19. and 20. The fruit you most dislike.
21. Your favourite months.

22. Your favourite accomplishment.
23. Your favourite periodical.
24. Your name and age.
25. Your residence and date.

----

1. O give me one brief hour of Wellington again,
2. Or crazed Lamancha's knight, of old chivalric Spain,
3. But speak not of the Neros, I loathe th' accursed name,
4. Or of Satanic Faust, lest blush the fiends for shame.
5. He is my favourite author who suits my changeful mood,
6. My favourite flower's the first blown primrose of the wood,
7. My favourite poet who first lured me to the skics,
8. But O there's no composer like a moping owlet's eyes.
9. I love the name of Emily, and gave it to my child.
10. At times I fancy Raphael, at times Salvator wild.
11. How charming on a sunny sea of Poesy to float,

12. How horrid to be sea-sick in a vile o'er-
    crowded boat !

13. My favourite dainty is a luscious lollypop.

14. Of the virtues I love best there grows no
    plenteous crop,

15. But the vices which I hate around like mush-
    rooms spring :

16. Then O " be just and fear not,"—a motto for
    a king.

17. My favourite pastime is to thin a young plan-
    tation,

18. My choicest fruit the apple when red as a car-
    nation :

19. None turns my stomach sooner than the bitter
    biting sloe ;

20. I know not that I have one, or I'd keep it for
    my foe.

21. I love the early summer months of May and
    leafy June,

22. And to hum dear " Auld lang syne," when the
    birds are all in tune,

23. Or to con the Quarterly. My name go seek
    on Teignmouth's shore.

24. On the shady side of seventy I dream of youth
    no more :

25. At Langton Hall in '67. Don't vote my
    rhymes a bore.

XXI.

ON HEARING A DISTINGUISHED DIPLOMATIST OB-
SERVE THAT THE SUCCESS OF OUR ABYSSINIAN
EXPEDITION HAD EXCITED MUCH JEALOUSY
ABROAD. MAY, 1868.

Now glory to the Lord of Hosts, and to England
    honour due :
What God hath wrought by British hands let none
    begrudging view.
Work waits on earnest will, nor lack brave deeds
    renown enew.
Then up at duty's call. Stout Austria cease thy
    griefs to rue ;
Nor Prussia while thy days are green for envy's
    sake turn blue :
Piece, gallant men of stars and stripes, the seam
    ye've rent in two;
And France a raid in Afric make, and a Duke of
    Timbuctoo ;
Grim Russia dare, where England shrank, nor
    Gallic eagles flew,

The blood avenging of our slain, and the wrongs
of Wolff the true.
And let our wounded sailor Prince his world-wide
cruise renew,
And crave the benediction of the Bishop of
Honolulu.
Quoth England to her sister states, "In time
there's nothing new,
And oh in space, beloved compeers, there's room
for me and you."

XXII.

THE THREE SISTERS;

A WELSH LEGEND.

The following lines, suggested by the recollection of a legend
which the author met with many years ago in Wales, were
composed during a visit to that country this year, 1869.

PLINLIMMON, king of mountains,
  Three nymphs he claimed his own
Tended the hallowed fountains
  That warbled round his throne.

I

And he thought they looked aweary,
  And fain, on wandering wing,
Beyond his moorlands dreary
  Would seek a brighter spring.

And he spake, albeit with sorrow
  Full laden was his heart,
That, on the coming morrow,
  For ever they might part :

And she, the earliest, shaking
  From her flowing locks the dews,
As prize of her awaking
  The goodliest lot might choose.

So while her sisters slumber
  Nor dream of wealth or power,
Fair Severn's vigils number
  Each slowly passing hour,

And the stars as they were fading
  O'er Snowdon's radiant brow,
His stalwart limbs o'ershading
  High hill and valley low.

But, grim and weather-beaten
  The ancient giant stood,
Nought in his looks to sweeten
  A maiden's changeful mood.

From Ocean darkly heaving,
  And from the shadowy screen
She turns, which woods are weaving,
  To the meadows' golden sheen.

In Apsley's gorge huge Wrekin
  Beholds a torrent gleam,
Malvern from either beacon,
  Mendip and distant Bream,

Mark on the exulting river
  Where mirrored sunbeams dance,
And, as from giant's quiver,
  Its arrowy currents glance,

And its tributary waters,
  As forth they roll in pow'r :—
The haughtiest of Earth's daughters
  Might covet such a dow'r.

Then rose old Ocean proudly
  The welcome nymph to greet ;
His surges sounding loudly,
  As when winds and waters meet.

And as when storms are brewing,
  Her clamorous warning gave
The sea mew of his wooing,
  As she heralded the wave,

Whose ebb and flow for ever
    Shall moons ordained renew;
That of that bridal never
    May fail memorial due.*

But now, bereft and weeping,
    Wye leaves her heathery bed,
To find, while she was sleeping,
    Her sister loved had fled.

From her watch-tower high and holy †
    She gazed with longing vain
O'er the moorland melancholy
    That bounds the western main.

But she saw in distance hazy,
    Where track'd the redd'ning sun
Her sister's footprints mazy,
    That her course was not yet run.

So forth she nimbly bounded
    To reach the distant shore ;
While caverned rocks resounded
    To the cataract's sudden roar.

---

* The lunar influence on the *bore* of the Severn and other
rivers has been lately questioned.
† Plinlimmon, a holy mountain.

Now softer tones are blending
  With the music of her march,
Where, her toilsome path descending
  The branching woods o'er-arch.

And now she fain would dally
  Where spreads the champagne fair,
And whitens the broad valley
  The blossom of the pear.

And now she lingers gladly
  Where ampler pastures bloom ;
Alas ! to rue more sadly
  The heedless loiterer's doom.

For though where cliffs are towering,
  Like one she speeds along
Who sees the tempest lowering,
  Or lists the siren's song,

Alas, till spell shall sever
  The Ocean's inmost brine,
The sisters twain shall never
  Their fond embrace entwine.

The sun had risen and brightly,
  But blanched what dire despair!
Young Isthwith's cheek, as lightly
  She trod the mountain bare.

So, through broken cloudland darting
    Adown the dizzy steep,
Marisch anð moss disparting,
    She rushes to the deep.

No pleasant nook embaying
    The eddying brooklet heeds,
No fragrant bower delaying,
    The headlong torrent speeds.

The vale she wins resistless;
    But, as to rue her haste,
Wanders forlorn and listless
    O'er the rough shingly waste;

Till, 'mid the wild commotion
    Of the ever-seething wave,
In the restless depth of Ocean
    She finds her lonely grave.

Traveller, thy name is Legion;
    From glaciers comest thou
Or Alpine or Norwegian,
    Or from Etna's burning brow?

Come, pay thine homage lowly,
    Ere the blithe lark carol yet
Upon the summit holy,
    Where sun and moon have met.

Drink of the hallow'd fountains
  As they sparkle in their glee,
Drink to the king of mouñtains,
  And to his daughters three.

———◆———

NORTH-RIDING BALLADS.

———

XXIII.

THE TIGER LILY:

NORTH-RIDING ELECTION.

JULY, 1865.

HURRAH for the Tiger Lily,
  Which the gallant Wallace* wore;
Hurrah! the Derby dilly
  Shall rule the realm no more.

'Twas on a July morning
  That of a coming fight
The trumpeters gave warning,
  In motley armour dight.

———

*. The late Lieut.-Gen. Sir Maxwell Wallace, K.C.H.

And led Northallerton's stout van
    A Chieftain, at his side
ˌ A heroine, like a stately swan
    Upon the swelling tide.

Welcomed loud cheers, while banners wave,
    Wallace of Waterloo,
And husky throats like welcome gave
    To his loyal lady too.

They met the portly Vicar,
    As he blandly strode along ;
And he spake, as his pace grew quicker,
    " Now, Lady, for a song."

" And would'st thou have me cater,"
    She said, " for such as thee,
To the good cause a traitor
    Of Yorkshire's liberty ? "*

Grimly the " Lion " ǀ he look'd down,
    From his palace of ale and gin,
While the landlord plied the thirsty town,
    And his jovial guests within.

---

* Electioneering chaff.
† The old " Golden Lion." Conservative head-quarters.

Quoth Wallace wight, with angry scowl,
" Thy sires and mine were foes,
And if I hear thy wonted growl
I'll twist thy Royal nose."*

The old " Black Bull " † claimed homage due,
As he marked the matchless pair ;
His eyeballs glared as they nearer drew,
And he tost his horns in air.

Then Wallace wight, with lowly bow,
" If thou our cause befriend,
A Golden Calf, none such, I trow,
To Parliament we'll send."

God prosper long yon solemn tow'r,
As when proud Surrey's host ‡
Wound past in Scotland's darkest hour ;
Be Church and State our boast.

But better suits yon mushroom spire
A creed of yesterday,
And those who would to power aspire
It boots not where they pray.

------

* Sir Maxwell was present as lineal representative of the
renowned Sir William Wallace, on the inauguration of the statue
of the great patriot in Scotland.
† Liberal head-quarters.
‡ To the battle of Flodden.

To lady fair and stalwart knight
A whisper came from far,
" Let not stern rule or modish rite
Betray the chance of war."

" Church and Dissent," quoth Wallace brave,
" To us are both alike,
When our country's wrongs our service crave,
And for the right we strike."

But ah, corrupt Northallerton,
Deaf to the charmer's voice,
And the cheer of Scotland's valiant son,
Thou bid'st the foes rejoice.

Now hark, what shout of victory
Awakes the drowsy street ?
Hath Milbank won,* and can it be
That we the victor greet ?

Yes, ere shall hymn the minster's knell
The requiem of the day,
Shall freedom's scathless citadel
The yellow flag display.

Hurrah for Milbank ! blessings shower
On him and those he led ;
Let Morritt seek his broken bower,
And Duncombe hide his head !

* North Riding Election.

Hurrah for the Tiger Lily,
Which the gallant Wallace wore ;
Hurrah ! the Derby dilly
Shall rule the realm no more.

———◆———

XXIV.

NORTHALLERTON'S LAMENT : ·

AFTER THE ELECTION :
AUGUST, 1865.

THEY gave me parchments* for a dower,
But ah the rifled cot,
And town that owns the foeman's power,
Are emblems of my lot.

Time was when 'mid the alders† rose,
That fringed my Sunnebecks' stream,
My fane‡ revered by friends and foes
Like fabric of a dream :

———

* Northallerton sent Members to Parliament in the 26th
Edward I.—*Ingledew's History of Northallerton.*
† Whence Northallerton derives its name.—*Ibid.*
‡ Built by Paulinus, A.D. 630.—*Ibid.*

When guileless innocence could frisk,
  Nor lovers tell a tale
Of ceaseless feud, where winds the Wiske,
  Or rolls the rushing Swale ;

When with my townsmen blent the throng
  Of Mowbray's rustics gay
To ply the mart, or swell the song
  Of sainted holiday ;

Or else in banded brotherhood,
  By crosier'd chieftains led,
Round the Holy Standard bravely stood,
  And for their country bled.*

But they are gone, the good old times,
  " The gallant days of old,"
To linger in the Church's chimes,
  Or haunt the breezy wold.

And lo for love, where'er we meet,
  Grim-visaged discord rife ;
In woodland path, or crowded street,
  We boast our civic strife.

And civic strife hath lofty aim,
  But few may reach its height,
While recreants claim the patriot's name
  And glory of the fight ;

---

* At the battle of the Standard, fought in the neighbourhood of
Northallerton.

Recreants who, when the conflict's o'er,
  Still cherish ranc'rous hate,
And still of public wrongs, while sore
  From paltry grievance, prate.

The honest tradesman these defraud,
  And pastor of his due,
Because forsooth he wears a gaud
  Of *Yellow* or of *Blue*.

These, skilled in party sophistry,
  Can tempt, to catch his vote,
The " rustic moralist " to " lie
  Most foully in his throat ;"

Or lure beguiled by false pretence
  Their victim from his post,
Or drench in bestial drink his sense,
  And of their knavery boast.

No more inspired by loyal trust,
  These spurn their country's call,
Inglorious as their arms that rust
  In mockery on the wall.

While orgies vile in God's own name
  Profane His sanctuary,
And chimes the live-long night proclaim
  Th' unhallowed revelry.

And do we truth and reverence scorn
For which our sires have bled?
Is there no living voice to warn,
Nor witness of the dead?.

Oh give me honour's troth again,
The bonds that bind the free :
Are fetters that the soul enchain
The badge of Liberty?,

----◆----

. XXV..
YELLOW FEVER.
NORTHALLERTON ELECTION BALLAD.
MAY, 1866.

PARODY ON THE CELEBRATED SONG, "ADMIRAL
·HOSIER'S GHOST."

*Scene.—Captain Peirse's House in Northallerton,
on the announcement by telegram of the success of
the Petition by which the Conservative Member
was unseated.*

WHEN the moon was brightly beaming
On Northallerton's old town,
At midnight with colours streaming
All triumphant we sat down ;

There while Johns, the Welshman, glorious
  From the Tories' late defeat,
And his voters, now victorious,
  Did their gallant leader greet;

On a sudden, shrilly sounding,
  The Teetotal Band was heard.;
Then each heart with fear confounding,
  A sad troop of ghosts appeared :
In faded yellow liveries shrouded,
  Which for winding sheets they wore,
And, with looks with sorrow clouded,
  Frowning where they smiled before.

On them gleamed the moon's wan lustre.;
  When the shade of Wrightson* brave
His pale ranks was seen to muster,
  And the yellow flag to wave :
O'er the glimmering stones he hied him
  To the house within the rai
In Zetland Street, his ghosts beside him,
  And did in groans the Welshman hail.

Heed, O heed my fatal story !
  I am Wrightson's injured ghost ;
Ye who now have purchased glory
  At this place where I was lost :

---

* In several Parliaments M.P. for Northallerton.

Though in Toryism's ruin
  You now triumph free from fears ;
When you think of my undoing
  You will mix your joy with tears.

See these mournful freemen reaping
  Fruit of priceless votes they gave,
Whose wan cheeks are stained with weeping ;
  These were honest tradesmen brave.
Mark those numbers pale and horrid,
  Who were once my Voters bold ;
Lo ! each hangs his drooping forehead,
  While his dismal tale is told.

I, by steadfast friends attended,
  Did the Tory town affright ;
Corruption nothing then defended
  But my orders not to fight.
O that in that fetid gutter
  I had cast them with disdain,
And with joy I could not utter
  Thrashed my ancient foes again !

For toil feared I none, or danger,
  But with trusty vet'rans had done
What thou, brave and happy stranger,
  Hast achieved with Peirse alone.

Then Conservatism never
  Had our foul dishonour seen,
Nor the links could treachery sever
  Which my joy and pride had been.

Thus, like thee, my foes dismaying
  I had struck, true Briton, home,
Though condemned for disobeying,
  I had met a mar-plot's doom :
To have fall'n, my country crying,
  " He has play'd an English part,"
Had been better far than dying
  Of a grieved and broken heart.

Unrepining at thy glory,
  Thy successful arms we hail ;
But remember my sad story,
  And let Wrightson's wrongs prevail.
While in dull repose I languish,
  Think what triumphs past in vain
This good town redeemed from anguish,
  From the Tories' hated chain.

Hence, with all my train attending
  From their foaming taps below,
Up the dear old street ascending
  Here I feel my constant woe.

Here the well-known sign-posts viewing
We recall our shameful doom,
And our plaintive cries renewing
Wander through the midnight gloom.

Up and down the highway mourning
Shall we roam deprived of rest,
To Northallerton returning,
But denied our just request ?
After the proud foe subduing,
When your patriot friends you see,
Think of your old Member's ruin,
And give place, my friend, to me.

XXVI.

THE OLD ROADSTER :

OR, THE NORTH-RIDING OF YORKSHIRE IN THE
19TH CENTURY.

A CHRISTMAS BALLAD, 1868.

The conflict lasting upwards of five years, which forms the
subject of the following Ballad, supplies one among many instances
of the deplorable consequences of the devolution of duty and of
responsibility by Ministers of State and Members of Parliament to
Courts of Quarter Sessions by what is called Permissive Legislation,
or in other words by no legislation at all.   Exceptional circum-
stances may justify the procedure ; but as a system it has proved

unconstitutional and degrading, and is not likely to survive the severe ordeal to which it has been already subjected.

The Old Highway Act was repeatedly, but unsuccessfully defended by Mr. Farsyde and other Magistrates, supported by a large body of Ratepayers, at the Northallerton Quarter Sessions, and on other public occasions.

It served moreover as a stalking horse to a third candidate, in the person of Mr. Cayley, at the late General Election, in defiance of a protest in a letter addressed by Mr. Farsyde to the Editor of the " Yorkshire Gazette," dated Fylingdale, Whitby Strand, 18th November, 1868, of which the following is an extract : " Has there been any spontaneous, any *felt* demand for Mr. Cayley's politics or his services ? Does he come forward as an original and natural opponent of the new Highway Act ? Certainly not. Col. Crompton, Captain Turton, and myself were its first, and with others its final opponents. Mr.' Cayley asserts he is an independent politician and farmer's friend. Electors, ask yourselves what these words mean ? Is Mr. Cayley more a friend to the farmers, more independent in politics, than either Mr, Milbank or Mr. Duncombe ? Do not his words mean that he desires to represent the Riding by an assumption of merit in connection with the Highway Act to which he is not entitled ?"

Mr. Farsyde is entitled to the pre-eminence assigned to him in the following lines, not only by the merit thus justly claimed, but by the energy and firmness which he has manifested during the protracted warfare, and his steadfast protest against the turbulent threats and misdoings of unscrupulous or foolish partisans.

On Whitby's Strand, slow-paced and sad,
  Sir Farsyde wends his way,
For ill hath fared the gallant pad
  That bore him many a day.

In brave antique heroic mould
  Sir Farsyde's soul was cast,
He loved the rugged paths of old
  The rude uncultured past :

The modern smooth highway he spurned,
  The modish gait and prim ;
The devious track he chose, nor turned
  Aside for perils grim.

And strange adventures he had sought,
  And earned hard-won renown,
On Whitby's strand with Mulgrave fought,
  And in many a leaguered town.

Around his banner mustered free
  The hardy sons of toil,
Who sink the shaft, or plough the sea,
  Or cleave the stubborn soil.

It dawns the day when each his fill
  Might quaff, nor longer rue
Base serfdom, master of his will,
  And of his neighbour's too.

For sage Sir Farsyde plainly saw,
  And taught his followers rough,
If each unto himself were law,
  There would be law enough ;

And so found quick solution
  Of mysteries of state,
While bloody revolution
  He held in deadly hate.

Then thus he spake : " When first I drew
  My falchion in the fight,
To heaven I vowed allegiance due,
  And eke to sceptered right.

Each in his sphere, tho' sworn to obey,
  May rule alternate, self
Concentering thus the sovereign sway,
  The nation's power and pelf.

Each township self-contained may prove
  The realm's epitome,
Submissive to the rule above,
  Yet uncontrolled and free :

As when along the dear old tracks
  Our rude forefathers trod
We jogged, unvexed by toll or tax,
  To mart or house of God :

Days when no prying pestering snob
  Could mar our festal cheer,
Nor ferret out each roguish job
  To rustic magnate dear ;

And no harsh churl unheeding past
  The poor man's outstretched hand,
Ere yet their baleful shadows cast
  Bastiles across the land."*

With loud acclaim the chief they greeted
  As he waved, on foundering nag,
Type of primeval roadster, seated,
  The old bucolic flag.

For he gazed on Mowbray's pleasant vale,
  Where wandering streams are blending,
Or winding Wiske, or rushing Swale
  From uplands drear descending ;

And marked where alders† still embower
  The famed historic nook,
Where rears Northallerton its tower
  O'er Sunnebeck's babbling brook.

And thither trooping warriors hie
  All shcathed in glittering steel,
And friends and foes list merrily
  The belfry's joyous peal.

---

* The able champion of Self Government, as exemplified in the
Old Highway Act, is here represented, by a poetic license, as the
exponent of the system in its more enlarged signification.

† Whence Northallerton derives its name.

And now the ranks are ordered,
   And spears are set in rest,
And loudly shouting " forward,"
   They're meeting crest to crest.

Clov'n helms and lances broken,
   And many a steedless knight
And palfrey riderless betoken,
   How fiercely fares the fight,

Where Johnstone, Thompson, and Straubenzee,
   And noble Zetland ply
Their flashing blades, while mid the frenzy,
   Brave " Duncombe " is the cry ;

Where Mulgrave stems the battle's tide,
   And Gallwey fain would form
His shattered files, and dim descried
   Young Worsley breasts the storm.

While he of Thornton hight le-Street,
   Of Cathcart's martial clan,
Now seeks repose in still retreat,
   Who once had led the van.

From smouldering stubble as the flame,
   Or shaft from bended bow,
Sir Farsyde to the rescue came,
   Nor conflict shunned the foe.

But soothing eve to festal cheer
Woos love—or—war-worn chief,
And home to generous hearts is dear,
So none chode parley brief;

While heralds shout, "A truce, a truce,
We part to meet again :
Hail foaming tap, the wine's rich juice,
The spirit-stirring strain!"

And truce to glory's cheating dreams:
On divers errands bent,
To acres broad, or moors, or streams,
The sated warriors went.

On Whitby's strand Sir Farsyde strode,
On Fylingdale's sweet grass
Browsed peacefully the steed he rode
Like any humble ass.

But where can rest be found? we ask,
And echo answers "Where?"
Again Sir Farsyde dons his casque,
And clamour rends the air.

He cries, "the fight is still unfought,
The triumph is not won;
Oh rally! or we're set at nought,
Proud deeds may yet be done."

Once more by Sunnebeck's babbling brook,
  And by the stately tower,
His way each eager chieftain took,
  While pealed the longed for hour.

And many a valiant heart beat high ;
  Their pennons who might number ?
For they knew that desperate is the die
  That wins the victor's slumber.

What champion leads the onset now ?
  Johnstone of Hackness, bold
As when he leads the chase, I trow,
  O'er Pickering's breezy wold :

While hostile Duncombe fires the war
  And Milbank, brethren twain,
Who once were foes ; and each from far
  Follows a goodly train.

Nor fails De Lisle in hour of need ;
  From Penshurst's storied towers
Full armed he comes,—fame wings his speed—
  And from Sidney's classic bow'rs.

Nor lack, though years his form have bent,
  Bland Yeoman's counsels sage,
Nor as volcanic fire long pent
  Dark Crompton's patriot rage.

Round Johnstone rallies many a knight :
Ne'er deaf to honour's call,
Foremost stout Zetland dares the fight,
Brave lord of Aske's high hall.

There sunny Langton's chief is seen ;—
He could tell many a tale
Of the dragon of his dell, I ween,
The fierce and foaming Swale :

Pulleine, whose studious leisure feeds
On quaint chivalric lore,
From Clifton's shades to match their deeds,
Who the Holy Standard bore. *

And lo ! may ne'er his banner droop,
The Lord of Bolton's lands
From Wensleydale, whence loyal Scrope
Led forth his archer bands.

Now " onward " was the password clear,
And dire the battle's shock.
From whose broad shield glance sword and spear,
Like breakers from the rock ?

------

* Mr. Pulleine selected in good taste, as the subject of a testi-
monial presented to him by his brother magistrates on retiring
from the Chairmanship of Quarter Sessions, the Battle of the
Standard, an event from which Northallerton derives historical
celebrity.

'Tis Whitby's chief, alas no more
His train-bands stout to lead :
All honour to the brand he bore,
And to his foundering steed ;

And honour to his spirit true
To England's Queen and laws ;
" No taunt deserved shall bid us rue
The people's righteous cause."

On Whitby's strand Sir Farsyde strode,
On Fylingdale's sweet grass
Browsed peacefully the steed he rode
Like any humble ass.

But hark ! what sullen sounds from far
The drowsy echoes wake ?
A monarch calls the realm to war,
A nation's weal 's at stake.

O'er moor and mountain, dale and down
Musters each thane his clan,
Each shopman spruce the marshalled town,
And well-skilled artizan.

Feuds, as his ranks each leader fills,
Are hushed as when the stream
The tempest's roar, or thunder stills
The clamorous seafowl's scream.

Twin battle cries the realm divide,
  Round banners twin apace
Gather the hosts, in severance wide,
  Stern foemen, face to face.

Sir Farsyde spake, while his heart beat high,
  And his palfrey answering neighed:
" Alas ! ill suits such revelry
 ' Thy shanks, my foundering jade."

Not thus Sir Cayley, " If my pluck,"
  Aside he spake, " in need
Fail not, in sooth I'll try my luck
  With this same gallant steed."

Then to his seat, his helm with blue
  And yellow plumage gay,
He vaulted, and a blast he blew
  To summon his array.

Cheers greeted him as on he rode,
  And the memory of his sire, *
And cheers the palfrey he bestrode,
  Tho' quenched his wonted fire.

----

* During many years M.P. for the North Riding.

In party-coloured pomp displayed
    He saw each line extend
Beneath the hallowed Minster's shade,
    While shouts the welkin rend.

What bosom thrills not when, all barred
    And bannered for the fight,
Lists in York's spacious Castle yard
    Are thronged with ladies bright ;

Where red-cross knights, renowned of eld,
    Where mighty Wentworth* strove,
And Helmsley's chief † the stirrup held,
    When lightened from above

His helm, and in Heaven's armoury wrought
    His scathless panoply,
Young Wilberforce triumphant fought
    That Afric might be free ;

---

* Earl of Strafford, afterwards beheaded, contested the County
of York in an election which produced stormy proceedings in Parliament.

† First Lord Feversham, grandfather of the present Earl,
Chairman of the celebrated Committee which ensured Wilberforce's election.

And wond'rous Brougham* of fame's sweet
    draught
Drank deeply, and when hoar
His brows, on tottering limbs here quaffed
    The nectared bliss once more.

Now hark the trump ! from yon dread keep
    The martial notes rebound ;
Ouse wafts responsive to the deep
    And hill to hill the sound.

Straight challenged to their saddle spring
    Two knights in tourney tried,
And brooking parlance brief the ring
    Two well matched champions ride.

But who is he on sorry brute
    Who fain the course would run,
His followers bannerless and mute
    For password they have none ?

" Give place," the heralds cry, " he bears
    A Cayley's honoured name,
Tho' motley be the suit he wears
    And he unknown to fame."

---

* Elected M.P. for Yorkshire.   He was enthusiastically received
on re-visiting the scene of his principal public triumph as President
of the Social Science Congress in 1864.

" Now stalwart chieftains, ere ye close,"
Sir Cayley spake, " in fight
I dare ye, mutual friends or foes,
Your sole or banded might."

But whence that shout ? what errand wings
That horseman's breathless speed ?
Tidings of joy or grief he brings,
Ye heralds true give heed.

For, soon as good Sir Farsyde found
That purloined was his pad,
On Whitby's strand his way he wound
With slow paced step and sad :

Then urged the swift pursuit, as dogs
The bloodhound staunch his prey,
O'er hills and dales, and wolds and bogs,
The hue and cry away.

Quick is the hare's prophetic ear,
The shy deer snuffs the wind,
The brave Sir Cayley knew not fear,
Nor reckt of foes behind.

But as at bay the stricken hart,
Whose flank the life blood dyes,
The yelling pack, the quivering dart,
And foremost foe defies,

At honour's call Sir Cayley flew,
　His steed so foundering lay :
Ah ! long the reckless knight shall rue
　The riding of that day.

But trumpets peace proclaim aloud,
　Wild shouts Sir Milbank greet,
And Duncombe's bands of triumph proud :
　No more as foes they meet.

Lo cynosure of sparkling eyes,
　Sir Duncombe 's victor crown'd :   .
Sir Milbank claims a second prize,
　Sir Cayley 's no where found.

Till thus Sir Milbank : " Thou thy fate
　Deserv'st, but not thy steed ;
His wayworn force I'll renovate,
　And eke repair his speed ;

And lieges he shall bear me well."
　Alas who hath not found
That warranty a horse may sell
　But cannot make him sound ?*

---

* Mr. Milbank upon the hustings declared his intention of
resuscitating the Old Highway Act.   Should he accomplish this
feat, he will deserve a burial where four roads meet at the expense
of the Ratepayers.

On Whitby's strand Sir Farsyde strode,
On Fylingdale's sweet grass
Fares well the foundered steed he rode
Like any humble ass !

XXVII.

CHURCH AND STATE.

LINES WRITTEN ON THE OCCASION OF A VISIT, IN
COMPANY WITH THE ARCHDEACON OF RICHMOND
AND ANOTHER REVEREND FRIEND, TO THE ANCIENT
SEAT AND SEPULCHRE OF THE MARMIONS AT WEST
TANFIELD, ON THE EURE. OCT. 13TH, 1868.

THE sunny slopes of Wensleydale
Are fair, and Clifton's bowers :*
'Tis sweet to muse o'er Eure's bright vale
Where stately Tanfield towers :

Where from yon ivied portal tall
Their wide-spread realm below
The Marmions, lords of Tanfield Hall,
Surveyed in weal or woe :

---

* Clifton Castle on the Eure.

L

Or sepulchred, all mail-clad, each
　His partner liege beside,
From marble lips unconscious teach
　A moral none may chide.

But other greeting waits us near,
　Where at his open door
The brave old pastor proffers cheer,
　And bids us dream no more.

And now within his sanctum snug,
　Where, in disorder rude,
Chairs, table, sofa, floor, and rug
　With parchments lie bestrewed,

Nor might unhallowed brush profane
　The honoured dust that there
Betokens well the lonely reign
　That no sweet nymph might share,

Marshalled we sat, each willing guest,
　While crowned the festal board,
Nor lacked wise saw nor frolic jest,
　The good man's choicest hoard.

And paid each churchman homage due
　A housewife staid and trim,
As foamed, for well her task she knew,
　The champagne o'er its brim.

The Archdeacon, while he smiled to see
  Such reverence, nothing loath,
Outdid the sparkling draught in glee,
  As he pledged us in his troth.

And pledged us, too, a priestly brother,
  And a Warden grave and sober,
And we thought, as still we pledged each other,
  Of the frost of chill October.

Then rose our venerable host,
  And pledged us all around,
As 'twere some wan unshriven ghost
  Had long-lost utterance found.

And we toasted the Marquis,* his patron,
  And the Bishop and cloistered lore,
And we toasted the cheery old matron,
  And we loved our Church the more.

And bound in staunch alliance,
  As well fledged our spirits rose,
We vowed point-blank defiance
  To our own and the Church's foes.

---

* Ailesbury.

While quivered every muscle,
  As we thought of fiendish Bright,
Sour Roebuck, crafty Russell,
  And Gladstone, traitor wight.

And we wished, and 'twas no wonder,
  For we had waxen bold,
He might be rent asunder
  Like his prototype of old.

And then, 'mid wild commotion
  Of the billow and the blast,
We tracked o'er Time's drear ocean
  The dark historic past.

But soon to sages curious
  Our dull task we consigned,
For we grew fast and furious,
  And none would lag behind.

Lay now the sunbeam level,
  And sprites at twilight roam,
So we thought to end our revel,
  And wend our way towards home.

And we toasted our good pastor,
  And we toasted Church and State,
And away we drove the faster
  For we knew that we were late.

And soon as, smiling grimly,
  We spied, athwart the gloom,
O'er the dusky city dimly
  The huge cathedral loom,

We praised the famous men of old,
  And our fathers who begat us,
And the Church whose banners we'd unfold
  Should the knavish Whigs be at us ;

And the solemn Convocation,
  And Ripon's goodly See,
And the Bishop's Visitation,
  Or Archdeacon's, as might be.

And should foes our vineyard trample,
  In Tanfield's hall again,
Toasting high each bright example,
  We'd seek no solace vain :

Or elsewhere, should have sealed stern fate
  The hospitable door,
We'd duly chronicle the date,
  And " drink to one saint more."

PARAPHRASES.

[XXVIII.

SOPHOCLES' "ELECTRA."

AND does this urn thy kindred dust enshrine,
Dear, lost Orestes, all that once was thine?
Bright as a star I sped thee from this land :
Now, ashes moulder in my trembling hand.
Ah! hadst thou died—ere rescued, but to prove
How vain a guardian's trust, a sister's love,
And on the day that sealed thy father's doom
Like honoured hadst thou shared his bloody tomb!
Alas! from home and from my care exiled
Thou fall'st, lorn outcast, on some desert wild :
These hands for thee no votive goblet filled,
Nor on thy corse the balmy draught distilled ;
But of thy form beloved what yet remains,
By strangers hallowed, this small urn contains.

XXIX.

VIRGIL : GEORGICS, IV., v. 453.

THOU rue'st—no dubious doom—the recompence
By heaven inflicted, of thy foul offence.

A husband's wrong the deadly curse inspires,
And Orpheus at thine hands his bride requires. `
In vain, in vain, thy guilty steps she fled,
As, ere she reached the river's long-sought bed,
Close-coiled the grassy bank's fierce guardian eyed
His victim, and the stream her life-blood dyed.

And rose from lofty Rhodope the wail
Of Dryad quires who wept her fate, the tale
Of woe Pangæum's crags and Geta far
Prolonging, and where sways the God of War
His Rhetian hills, and Orithyia lone,
And surging Hebrus' melancholy moan.

But Orpheus mourning paced the desert shore,
His lyre the burden of his anguish bore ;
And still to thee, loved spouse, its cords were
    strung,
Ere the faint dawn its earliest lustre flung ;
And still to thee attuned its latest lay,
As died the light on western waves away.

Now unappalled, impelled by frenzied love,
He dares the gloomy horrors of the grove,
That hides from mortal ken th' infernal gate
Where Tænarus lowers, and Pluto's kingly state—
Regions unblessed, the Manes' dread abode,
Dominions of th' inexorable God.

Moved by the lyre's sweet minstrelsy, around
The spectres wan of Erebus profound
Swarm, as the feathered myriads throng the wood,
When ev'ning wooes or swells the wintry flood,
Matrons and sires, and mighty heroes slain,
Virgins who sighed for earthly loves in vain,
And youths by hands parental to the pyre
Consigned ; while round the reedy shores, through
    mire
And slimy sedge, Cocytus wanders slow,
And the loathed Stygian streams in nine-fold
    circles flow.

Hell from beneath is roused : Death's sullen ear
Startles the unwonted sound : the Furies rear
Their serpent locks : mute at the gate of Death
Hell's three-mouthed watchdog holds his labouring
    breath,
And bends, oblivious of immortal woes,
Ixion from his wheel in grim repose.

And scathless from the perils of the way
Now panted Orpheus on the verge of day ;
And still his steps, so Proserpine decreed,
Eurydice pursued with faithful speed :
When, oh ! what dire illusion mocks his sense—
Could Hell forgive, how venial the offence !—

What spell o'erpowers the lover's constant mind!
He yields, and casts a wistful look behind.
In token of the forfeit, thunders shake
Thrice pealing from its depths th' Avernian lake :
While to her Orpheus thus the frenzied bride :
" What madness blasts our rescued bliss ? " she
    cried,
" Again I hear the Fates' resistless call,
And on my swimming eyes Death's slumbers fall;
The gathering shadows round their victim twine,
Ah ! meet my fond embrace, alas, no longer
    thine ! "
She spake, and, as a vapour melts in air,
Vanished, unconscious of his mute despair,
While fondly still he clasped the empty shade,
And many a sign of speechless anguish made :
And could no vows restore his twice-lost love,
Nor prayers the Gods, nor tears the Manes move ?
Ah, no ; the death-boat to the Stygian coast
E'en now hath borne the unreturning ghost.

Deep in the dark recesses of a cave,
Where rocks aërial frown o'er Strymon's wave,
For seven long months, as legends tell, his groan
Orpheus renewed, unpitied and alone ;
Till woods drew near enraptured as he sang,
And tigers owned the spell that soothed his pang.

In poplar shades unseen, till dawns the day,
Her unfledged brood, of some rude churl the prey,
So mourns the nightingale, while o'er the vale
Thrills the sad descant of her oft-told tale.
His grief no Hymeneal rites beguiled,
Nor Venus on the bard benignant smiled :
But where, 'mid hyperborean wastes afar,
On freezing Tanais gleams the northern star,
Or where on cold Ryphæum's mountains drear
The sleety tempests chafe the wintry year,
A wanderer lone th' eternal snows he trod,
And rued the vain relentings of the God ;
Till, as he spurned their proffered love, inspired
By jealous rage, to slay the bard conspired
Cyconia's matrons.   And his mangled limbs
Revealed, while pierced night's silent noon the
    hymns
Of frantic Bacchanals, the deed of blood.
And while his severed head adown the flood
Of Hebrus, foaming o'er the Œagrian plain,
The whirling eddies tost, the wonted strain
Still lingered on his lips and faltering tongue,
As still the lost Eurydice he sung :
Eurydice his parting spirit sighed—
Eurydice the rocks and hollow shores replied.

XXX.

HORACE.

Book 2nd. Ode 10th.

Shape well thy course, Licinius, why
    Thus ever rashly tempt the deep,
Or when the storms appal thee, fly
    Where vainly warns the threatening steep ?

Contentedly a humble lot,
    Life's golden mean who fain would choose,
Nor grovelling penury's squalid cot,
    Nor wealth's much envied grandeur rues.

Winds the tall pine assail, the tower
    That's loftiest falls with heaviest shock,
And quivering owns the Thunderer's power
    The blasted summit of the rock.

Mindful of change, the steadfast soul
    Sorrows with hope, exults with fear;
Jove bids the winters onward roll,
    Then vanish from the vernal year.

The ills, too, of the day shall end :
    Apollo shall again inspire
The slumbering muse, nor always bend
    The bow that bears his treasured ire.

Boldly the gathering storm await;
Then shall thy readier hand restrain
The swelling sails, when happier Fate
Propitious lulls the boisterous main.

———◆———

XXXI.

HABAKKUK.

CHAPTER 3RD.

I HEARD Thy voice, O God, with thrilling fear:
Lord of Eternity, while year to year
Succeeds, revive Thy work, Thy will declare,
In wrath remember mercy, Lord, and spare.

The Holy One from lofty Teman came;
And Paran bowed beneath His car of flame,
O'er Heaven's deep vault a flood of glory poured,
And Earth's hosannahs loud His name adored.
Invisible, in brightest beams arrayed,
While round His outstretched arm the lightnings
    played,
In shrouded majesty th' Almighty rode,
And fire and pestilence before Him flowed.
He stood to mete the Earth : no eye might brook
His glance revealed : the nations fled, and shook
The everlasting hills : none else might span
The Infinite's unchanged and changeless plan.

In Cushan's tents is heard the voice of wail,
And guilty Midian's ancient bulwarks fail.
Why on the rivers burst Thy treasured wrath?
Did vengeance urge Thee on Thy billowy path,
When horse and chariot clave the parting main?
Nor was Thy bow unsheathed, or promise vain.

Forth rushed the rivers from the opening sod,
And mountains trembling owned a present God,
And flung the deluge in its boundless sweep
Its foam on high, and answered deep to deep;
While sun and moon in either lessening sphere,
Shrank from Thine arrowy sheen and glittering
    spear.

O'er land and sea triumphant, as the flail
Winnows the chaff, Thou bad'st the heathen quail,
And Thine anointed hail thy saving power,
When quivered to its base the smitten tower,
Nor refuge found their mightiest when Thy foes,
To oppress the poor, like whirlwind blast arose.
Triumphant was Thy step on land and sea,
Through the walled waves Thy chariots bounded free.
I heard the trampling of Thy steeds, confest
My lips the anguish of my lab'ring breast,
And my bones quaked, ah, lest, on that dread day,
Appalled I share Thy flying foes' dismay.

Albeit no vernal bloom the fig-tree bear,
Nor purple vintage crown the waning year,
No fruit the olive in its season yield,
Nor golden harvest load the teeming field,
The shepherd swain with weeping eye behold
The stall forsaken and the empty fold,
Yet in the Lord my God will I rejoice,
For His salvation raise my grateful voice,
And by His might restored my strength renew,
Fleet as the hart that drinks the morning dew.

SWIFT and Co., 55, King Street, Regent Street, W.

www.ingramcontent.com/pod-product-compliance
Lightning Source LLC
Chambersburg PA
CBHW020011030726
47500CB00002B/535